**“No!” Luvell**
throat dramaticall
*getting to those me..* I...mean, I may not announce this to the group just yet. When I get a few free minutes at the store tomorrow, I’ll come over to find out the railroad’s decision.” She pushed one long curl back into the ribbon again. “Thank you, Mr. Johannson,” she said, using her low voice and smiling. “It’s a pleasure doing business with you.”

She turned into the wind, which suited her mood perfectly, soaring and exhilarating and powerful, as Mr. Johannson went into the depot. She almost floated over to the Muncy Inn, where her best friend, Anna, was waiting for her. Anna was the only other person, besides Steckie and Bessie, who knew about what she planned for the caboose.

Inside the inn lobby, Anna’s father was sitting in his office behind the registration counter glowering at some papers. The smell of his cigar mingled with that of fried bacon wafting in from the Smythe family’s quarters in the back.

Anna pulled Luvella into a small sitting area off the lobby. “Oh, tell me, Luvella. Quickly!” She held both of Luvella’s hands in her own.

“I think I did it, Anna! I think I did it!”

## Author's Note

Although my research for this novel has been thorough, and I have a lengthy bibliography, this is a work of fiction. I have taken liberties with the layout of Muncy Valley so it supports the needs of the story, particularly the bonanza and football game. The football game is completely fictional, although Jim Thorpe was indeed on his way to the Stockholm Olympics at the time. (In actuality, I'm sure Pop Warner would never have allowed any of his players to participate in a sandlot game like the one in this story.)

Although my research discovered a Native American presence, especially in the early Forksville area, my story probably includes a stronger influence than actually occurred. However, many Native Americans stayed, very quietly, as close to their lands as possible after our government transferred their children from their homes to industrial schools to train them in "white man's" ways, language, clothing, and culture and tried to move all Natives to reservations. The Delawares had called that area of Pennsylvania home for many, many years. Muncees was a tribe within the Delaware Nation. I have to say, this is not one of our country's proudest moments.

Although *Luvella's Promise*, the children's prequel to this novel, is based on many stories my mother had told me about her growing up in Muncy Valley, this story, *The Heartbeat of the Mountain*, is pure and complete fiction.

Any errors in historical and/or geographical data are completely mine and not from any of the learned suppliers of my research or my editor or publisher.

# The Heartbeat of the Mountain

by

Joan Foley Baier

This is a work of fiction. Names, characters, places, and incidents are either the product of the author's imagination or are used fictitiously, and any resemblance to actual persons living or dead, business establishments, events, or locales, is entirely coincidental.

**The Heartbeat of the Mountain**


Contact Information: info@thewildrosepress.com

Cover Art by *Tina Lynn Stout*

The Wild Rose Press, Inc.
PO Box 708
Adams Basin, NY 14410-0708
Visit us at www.thewildrosepress.com

Publishing History
First American Rose Edition, 2017
Print ISBN 978-1-5092-1387-0
Digital ISBN 978-1-5092-1388-7

Published in the United States of America

**Dedication**

To Jack, Bruce, and Tom
who are my warriors

## Acknowledgments

This book has been years in the making and then more years of submitting to various publishers and finally, selecting from the short list of publishers who had accepted my manuscript. And the list of people to whom I owe much is a long one.

In my research process, I visited the Muncy Valley, Pennsylvania area several times, my early visits for information and data primarily for the prequel to *The Heartbeat of the Mountain*, *Luvella's Promise*. The people in Sullivan County were so friendly and helpful, I discovered there was another story about Luvella, and that is how *The Heartbeat of the Mountain* was born.

On one of my visits there, I, and my mother who is the inspiration for Luvella, participated in a book signing at Kathleen Nelsen's Katie's Country Store (now under different management) when she hosted a Basket Bonanza. It was a festive occasion, and although her store was the only one having it, the sale was a major incentive for me to make it an integral activity in my Heartbeat novel. Kathleen graciously gave me permission to use the sale title in my story, and generously included her statement that she "has no monopoly or claim to the words." Thank you, Kathleen.

The folks at *The Sullivan Review*, the museums in Dushore and Eagles Mere, and the Visitors Center in Muncy Valley were all so eager to help. Marianne Frasier of the Council on the Arts in Sullivan County was a wealth of information. Also the Wyalusing, Pennsylvania Eastern Delaware Nations Cultural Center kindly welcomed my mother and me into their new, at that time, center and even invited us to an upcoming pow-wow. Another year, I was invited to share in the Forksville Festival for a book signing, along with storytellers and exhibits of their Native American heritage. My heartfelt gratitude goes to all of you.

Many thanks must go to my early readers: Margie Hillenbrand, Sue Murphy, Sheri Gumina, and Cynthia Bassett. Their patience, suggestions, and insights inspired me to continue that long, lonely journey through writing a novel.

Football is not one of my pursuits, vicariously or otherwise. I had to do considerable delving to get the feel of a game. When I finally put one together on paper, my grandson, Brian Page, reviewed it thoroughly and saved my life more than once in the process. Thanks, Brian!

Much appreciation and recognition for their professional input on horses, their behaviors, care, reactions, stamina, and everything horsey go to Gwenn Green and Jackie Paterson.

Working with my editor, Allison Byers, has been a joy, and I appreciate so much her input and corrections. I'm a lover of exclamation points, which became very obvious to me when I saw her delete them, one by one. Thank you, Allison, for a great job, well done. And I'd like to thank the president of Wild Rose Press, Rhonda Penders, also, for her patience and professional management.

My family, of course, is always and forever providing all-round support in my writing endeavors and my granddaughter, Brittany Touris, is my trusted sounding board. Thank you! And finally, to Paul Vail, who encouraged me constantly to keep writing and accompanied me on my most recent research foray to

Muncy Valley and Sullivan County: rest in peace, Paul.

## Chapter One

*Muncy Valley, Pennsylvania*
*1912*

A sudden gust of summer wind held her hostage, as if in warning. She shook her head, chin up, feeling a curl of her hair pull loose from the large white bow in back. *That dream is spooking me. But I know what I'm doing, and I need the caboose to do it.* She turned around to look up at the mountain, its pines nodding in the breeze. *Besides, my mountain stands strong with me.* Nothing *is going to scare me away.*

She thought she saw a movement—something brown—in the woods close to the road. *Probably a deer.*

She continued walking down the mountain road, avoiding the wagon ruts and the tiny rivulets of ochre water running down them from last night's rain. As she remembered the rain beating against her bedroom window, waking her to her dream, a shiver rippled through her.

*Oh my goodness, Luvella. Stop being so dithery. You have to concentrate on your purpose this morning.*

Behind her, a scuff! She began to turn when an arm suddenly wrapped around her neck, pulling her backward. A dirty hand, smelling of tobacco, covered her mouth and stifled her scream. She closed her eyes and bit hard on the disgusting hand. She pulled at his arms and kicked his leg. He yanked her neck tighter. She could hardly breathe.

He bent back, bending her also and lifting her feet from the ground. He pressed his head close to hers. His whiskers brushed against her cheek as he growled into her ear, “Lissen here, little filly. Stay away from that caboose if you know what’s good for ya.”

“I told ya she’d be a hussy,” a second man hissed from the woods near the road. “But Rusty said not to hurt her.”

“Shut up!” the man holding her snarled. He lifted her even higher, squeezing her ribs until she thought they would crack. Then he threw her to the ground. She landed on her hands and knees. Like a rag doll, her head jolted forward and hit the dirt road. She grunted like an old man from the impact.

She felt like Mr. Melk’s hammer had struck her knees, smashing them through to the backs of her legs. Her hands burnt, and she was sure they had been pushed right up to her elbows. At the same time, the sounds of snapping twigs and something pushing through brush told her the two men were running away. She coughed as dust and mud swirled into her face and up her nose. Oddly, she could see her reticule lying perfectly on the road, as if she had laid it there. Nothing had fallen out—not her comb, her white lace-trimmed handkerchief, or even her hairpins.

White spots danced behind her eyes. She forced her arms—her hands were still where they belonged—to push herself up from the road, to her tortured knees, and to her feet. Her head pounded; her forehead burnt from hitting and scraping against the road; her neck felt battered.

She threw furtive glances in all directions. No signs of those men, but she didn't want to dawdle.

She looked at the front of her white cotton dress. "Oh, no-o—o!" she cried. She brushed off much of the dusty mess, but where her legs had rubbed into the road, there were darker smudges. On her arms, too. She looked back up the road to where her house was.

*No. Mama would faint dead away if she saw me like this. I'll go to Bessie's.*

She limped down the road and soon turned left onto Main Street.

The street stretched before her; off to the right was the road leading to Daddy's sawmill. The scene straight ahead, seeming to change every day according to the weather, always caught her breath. Today she just welcomed it, the safety of it.

Under clouds buffeted by the wind, the buildings in their muted shades of grays and blues and barn-red prompted an image of Mama's current patchwork quilt project. When the sun peeked through, the colors brightened, and the contours were more clearly defined—the blue cottage look of Muellers' house-ice cream store-post office, the prim brown of Mrs. Kiergen's sewing store and her upstairs apartment, the deep red of the train depot. Her line of vision stopped there. That was her destination. But first, she turned left into Bessie's house.

When she opened the door, her sister's smile changed immediately to shock. "Luvella! Get in here! What on earth happened to you?"

Bessie led her younger sister to the kitchen table and gently pushed her onto a chair. "Your face! What happened to your face? And your neck! It's all red and looks like it's going to bruise." She grabbed one of Vanessa's diapers and pumped water on it, wringing most of the water out. "Luvella Andersson, tell me everything right now!"

As Bessie ministered to her, Luvella relayed what had happened and what the men had said. And as she reviewed the scene, she felt the full weight of it, the threat of it, the danger to her. Her eyes overflowed, and she struggled to stay calm. She didn't want to wake Bessie's baby.

"Well," Bessie said, "even though you won't be seeing Mr. Johannson today, you *will* be working at the store. We can dab some powder on that brush burn on your forehead and let me get that old gingham dress I wore before Junior was born and I was thin, like you. You can wear that today while I wash and iron this dress."

"Oh thank you, Bessie. You're a blessing. But I am definitely going to my meeting with Mr. Johannson. And I am definitely going to rent that caboose."

After making Bessie promise to not tell Mama or Daddy about those men, she continued her determined walk down Main Street, only slightly favoring her right leg. Her long skirt billowed with the wind. She scowled. *Sometimes skirts can be such a bother. I bet I could have run away from those men in a shorter skirt.* Halfway into her sixteenth year and her first year to wear ankle-length dresses, she still longed for the freedom of the shorter version.

She waved at Mrs. Kiergen, who was arranging a dress in her store window. Luvella was careful to show only the good side of her face. Then she recommenced her brisk pace past Steckie's Hardware store and its front corner where her gift business resided. As she walked, her eyes sought the old caboose, deteriorating in the lot between Steckie's and the train depot. It stood amidst tall grass and weeds, like an old cow in a wheat field, and possessed none of the splendor Luvella hoped to bring to it.

She studied the flaking dark red paint on its west side, the cracked glass, the back door, which faced the front of the lot and would be her front entrance, with the curtain on only one of its twin windows. She knew from her previous inspection that the interior was in just as much neglect. *Why do those men want this wreck of a building? They certainly don't seem like businessmen.*

She scanned the yard, her eyes resting momentarily on the privy in back, between the caboose and the depot.

*Aha.* If this had been a better morning, she would have chuckled. *Mr. Johannson has had it painted very recently. So, he* is *interested in renting this to me.*

She closed her eyes to see her vision of success, to see her future here, and if she planned right, the prosperous future of Muncy Valley. Little Muncy Valley, in northern Pennsylvania, thriving. Groups of people, filling the shops and businesses—especially *her* crafts business—and walking the boardwalk, which she had urged the merchants to install last year. Another idea she'd taken from reading *Harper's Magazine.*

A cloud-driven shadow skulked across her vision. She stared at the door. *Something...Something else about that caboose...* Her dream surfaced again, the view of the caboose pulling away, that tall man emerging in a threatening stance onto its back platform.

Goosebumps prickled the back of her neck. But more determined than ever, she walked past the old railroad car to the train depot and her meeting with Mr. Johannson, the railroad's manager and her key to the caboose.

At the stoop to the depot, she stopped. *I have to act like a businessman. This is my last chance to stand up to him.* Then she tucked her errant hair into the tied ribbon, squared her shoulders, and brightened her face with a confident smile. She stepped up and opened the door.

Mr. Johannson stood when she entered the depot. *That's good. He's finally treating me like a grown lady.*

"Good morning, Luvella," Mr. Johannson said formally between lips stretched in a cursory grin. He held in his hand a short piece of wood, to which keys were attached, and tapped it against his leg. "You're sure about this?"

*He's nervous, too.* "Absolutely," she said. "But I'd like to see it again."

Mr. Johannson peered at her, squinting his eyes. "What happened to you, Luvella?"

"Oh, bumped into the doorway in the dark last night," she lied.

She followed Mr. Johannson out of the depot, taking long strides to match his and counting them…*nine, ten, eleven. About thirty feet. An easy passage for the train travelers to enjoy a little shopping.* She couldn't help it. She smiled. But climbing the five steps to the back platform and into the abandoned railroad caboose, she hesitated and gripped the framework of the door. The cool, dank air raised the hairs on her arms and prickled her scalp, feeling like ants crawling through her hair.

*That dream haunts me. And those men... I have to figure out who that man was in my dream. And I wonder if he's connected to those men.* She studied the man before her. *Maybe Mr. Johannson?* His head almost touched the car's ceiling. *He's tall, too, but he just doesn't have that...that evil air about him.*

He peered down at her, his brows pinched together. "Are you reconsidering, Luvella? You look worried."

"I was thinking about all the work this will need," she said, cloaking her fears with the little lie.

"Well-ll," Mr. Johannson replied. "I've been thinking, too. I haven't seen your daddy here yet. When will he want to see it? He'll have to give his consent, y'know."

Luvella lowered her head and turned away from Mr. Johannson. Ignoring his question, she strolled down the aisle. She stopped halfway down, sensing Mr. Johannson right behind her. Then, filling her chest with air and resolve, she turned sideways to the manager. She reached out to run her fingers over some of the gouges in the benches along the wall and traced the cracks in one of the windows. She squinted to look out a second cracked window and tugged at the back door's cloth curtain, which fell into her hand, while Mr. Johannson shifted feet and cleared his throat.

Luvella began, "I've developed a large clientele in the Valley and with the few tourists who come through." That word, clientele, would impress Mr. Johannson. "Of course, you are aware my ideas and advertising—from reading my *Harper's Magazine*—brought the tourists here in the first place. Indeed," she continued in her lofty tone, "I'm the one who talked all our merchants into forming an association for our own benefit as well as for the Valley's." She took a breath and finished, "You know I can pay the rent."

"This here's hard for me, Luvella." Mr. Johannson, still nodding in agreement, scratched his head. "I have to answer to the railroad, y'know."

"Yes, I understand, Mr. Johannson." She lowered her voice to sound older, and serious-minded. She had to make this work and now was the moment. "Have you told them my name yet?"

"Well-l-l, no," he said. "I only said someone was interested. If I wired them the interested person was just a girl, they'd laugh me offa the telegraph." He let out a squeaky laugh. He was nervous now, worried he might lose her business after all.

Apparently, those men hadn't contacted him yet about the caboose, and she wanted to finish this before they did. So, very slowly, she peered at each of the dilapidated furnishings and walls, frowning at the one hole behind the desk. She winced as she opened the stove's door, which screeched in rebellion.

Something different was there, and she bent to peer inside, her right knee reminding her of that man's attack. She stood back and invited Mr. Johannson to look. She didn't say a single word.

He reached into the cold stove and brought out two jugs. He pulled the corks and sniffed.

"Moonshine," he barely whispered. "Someone's been in here."

Although Luvella was pretty sure she knew who had been inside the caboose, she didn't say. She could *feel* Mr. Johannson's confidence wavering as he fidgeted with the jugs and made that whistling noise as he breathed. At the entrance to the car, she turned abruptly, swishing her skirt, to face him.

"Mr. Johannson." She tried to keep her heart from sounding like a train in a tunnel. "Since the W and NB Railroad is already interested, you can tell them that you have L. Andersson wanting to rent this caboose for seven dollars a month. You don't have to mention whether L. Andersson is a man or a bear—just L. Andersson."

Opening the door, she steadied her hands on the grab rail, stepped down the stairs to the ground, and braced against the rising wind. "I'd like to have this…arrangement…completed by next week," she said, hoping he didn't hear the quaver in her voice. "Can you please do that for me, Mr. Johannson?" She used all her inner strength to smile up at him.

He blushed, clearly feeling put upon, and kept tapping his fingers on the jugs. It seemed like hours passed before he finally spoke. "Luvella, let's see what I can do. I'll have the answer for sure by our merchants' group meeting tomorrow and can let you know then."

"No!" Luvella blurted, and then cleared her throat dramatically. *I don't want any news of this getting to those men.* "I…mean, I may not announce this to the group just yet. When I get a few free minutes at the store tomorrow, I'll come over to find out the railroad's decision." She pushed one long curl back into the ribbon again. "Thank you, Mr. Johannson," she said, using her low voice and smiling. "It's a pleasure doing business with you."

She turned into the wind, which suited her mood perfectly, soaring and exhilarating and powerful, as Mr. Johannson went into the depot. She almost floated over to the Muncy Inn, where her best friend, Anna, was waiting for her. Anna was the only other person, besides Steckie and Bessie, who knew about what she planned for the caboose.

Inside the inn lobby, Anna's father was sitting in his office behind the registration counter glowering at some papers. The smell of his cigar mingled with that of fried bacon wafting in from the Smythe family's quarters in the back.

Anna pulled Luvella into a small sitting area off the lobby. "Oh, tell me, Luvella. Quickly!" She held both of Luvella's hands in her own.

"I think I did it, Anna! I think I did it!"

# Chapter Two

Anna and Luvella hugged each other, jumping up and down, stepping back to look at each other, and then hugging again. "I just know I am actually going to have my store in the caboose. I imagine Mr. Johannson's tapping that Morse code message on the wires to the railroad right this minute."

"Oh, Luvella. I'm so happy for you." Anna sat on the velvet chair across from the love seat and leaned forward to whisper. "When are you going to tell your mama and daddy?"

Luvella rested an elbow on the arm of her chair and pressed her hand to her forehead. "I'll ask Bessie for some ideas on my way home from the store today. But I don't want to tell anyone else until I know it's for sure and I'm ready." She looked at Anna. "Another business could come along and offer Mr. Johannson more money.

"As a matter of fact, Anna, two men attacked me on my way down my road and warned me against getting the caboose. And we found some moonshine in the stove there. I'm sure those men left it."

Mr. Smythe coughed and cleared his throat. Anna's eyes followed the sound to his office. She leaned toward Luvella, speaking softly. "Luvella, now *you* have to keep a secret for me." She lowered her voice even more. "Some nasty man was in here two weeks ago and came in again today. Daddy's been ornery and going over those bookkeeping records ever since." Tears welled in her eyes and her voice wavered. "I think Daddy…might be losing the inn."

Luvella covered Anna's hand with her own. "I am so sorry, Anna. But remember just two years ago how my whole family—'cept me—had typhoid fever and how we lost the sawmill and our house. Now, I have my business and Daddy has the sawmill back."

"I know," Anna replied. "But this man seems so"—she shook her head for emphasis—"so *determined* to take over the inn and push Daddy out. With that depression in ought-seven and then the typhoid epidemic, the inn has been…almost empty."

Luvella glanced out the window, studying the caboose. *That feeling again…every time I see the back of the caboose.* She turned slowly to face Anna. "Is this man quite tall, with red hair and a beard?"

Anna nodded, her head bobbing repeatedly. "And mean eyes."

"He was in the store a couple weeks ago, in and out," Luvella murmured, "and he kept touching things, like he wanted *them*, too." She looked out at the caboose again. *What is in my head that wants to come out?* "He asked Steckie about your inn. In fact, Anna, I slightly recollect seeing him somewhere else besides my store but can't remember where."

Anna's shoulders raised almost to her ears, then returned to normal as she let out a long sigh. "We need some visitors to town, Luvella. If I have to move away, we might never see each other again. You're so good at advertising the Valley. If you think of something new, I'd be glad to help you with it."

"Now you're thinking," Luvella said. "I haven't read the latest *Harper's Magazine,* but the new issue came in yesterday. I'll take one home with me today. And now," she said as she walked toward the door, "I have to get to the store."

When Luvella entered the hardware store, Steckie smiled. "How was your meeting? You look right happy."

Luvella twirled, her hands reaching skyward, her head tilted back. "I think I have it, Steckie." Then she told him how she gave the name for Mr. Johannson to use, and Steckie chuckled.

"Luvella, I'm glad you're my sister-in-law, and not a competitor. You're so much like my little wife." They both laughed.

"I want to stop and see Bessie on my way home, Steckie—tell her my news. Any sales while I was gone?"

Steckie pulled his brows together. "As a matter of fact, that tall gentleman came back—right after I saw you walk past the store. He sashayed directly over to your display case and inspected everything, carefully. It was as if he knew you weren't here. Did you see him?"

Luvella shook her head and strode quickly behind her display case, checking her stock as if she thought he had run off with something.

"He bought Thirza Maarten's quilt," Steckie continued, awe strengthening his voice. "The most expensive item in your inventory."

Luvella was contemplating that—the thrill of the big sale and the menace of the steely-eyed buyer—when Steckie added in a quiet tone, "He said he's coming to our meeting tomorrow."

"He's coming?" she shouted in a shrieky whisper. "He's *coming?*" She turned and paced behind the case. "Why? Did you invite him? How did he know about our group? How did he know about the meeting?"

"Whoa, Luvella! I didn't tell him anything. He said he'd met with David Smythe. And then he said since he will soon be the new owner of the inn, he thought it would be important for him to meet the other businessmen here in the Valley. David Smythe gave him the partic'lars."

"Steckie, there's something evil about that man."

"I know what you mean. Bessie said the same thing when she saw him. But we shouldn't…listen too hard to our suspicions."

Luvella just turned her head from side to side. "But oh. I don't want him to be there."

****

At five o'clock, Luvella picked up the latest issue of *Harper's Magazine* from her new magazine rack and rushed toward home. She stopped at Bessie and Steckie's house situated near the road leading up the mountain to her own home. When she knocked and entered, Bessie greeted her with a big hug. "Oh, Luvella, I just finished ironing your dress."

"Bessie, you are the best big sister ever. And I have some news, so it's a good excuse to put our elbows on the table together, as Mama always says. Where's Vanessa?"

"She's taking a late nap. It'll be a long night tonight." But she smiled and her eyes glistened like morning sunshine.

After Luvella changed back into her own dress, they sat at the table in the kitchen, hugging their cups of coffee. Luvella reached to squeeze Bessie's hand. "I had my meeting with Mr. Johannson. I think he's going to help me get the caboose. I hope to start cleaning it next week."

Bessie's eyes opened wide. "Oh my land! I didn't know it would happen so soon."

Luvella smiled. She loved Bessie's natural exuberance as much as her keen business mind.

Bessie added, "We can all help you. I can bring Vanessa in her basket, and we can get it ready just like we did for your corner of Steckie's store. What did Mama and Daddy say about it?"

Luvella shifted in her chair. "They don't know yet, Bessie. And I really don't know how to tell them."

"You'll figure out how," Bessie said. "But you should do it right away."

"I will. I promise," Luvella said. "I was hoping you'd have a suggestion about how to begin, at least." When Bessie just rolled her eyes, Luvella laughed, stood, and took her coffee cup to the sink. "Speaking of Mama, I'd better get home. She's still tired from the pneumonia. It's hard to see her so exhausted."

Luvella clutched the magazine under her arm and stepped off the front porch. She glanced down Main Street and stopped abruptly. There, stepping out of the bank and onto the street, the tall, red-headed man turned to walk up Renter's Run, the road leading to the tenant houses. He hesitated, putting something inside his jacket, and then walked on. Even though he was tall and slender, Luvella thought he had the look of a fat mountain lion licking his chops. She frowned and turned to rush up the mountain road to her home, peering deep into the woods all about her.

Later she'd surely have to tell Daddy about the two men. But first, she would tell Mama, when she was home and alone with her.

The fog had lifted, even though the sun remained filtered behind clouds. But Luvella could see her mountain—Pennsylvania's North Mountain—and feel the warmth of the sun, and her mood was aloft. Since she was busy planning her evening—read *Harper's*, think of new advertising ideas, and how to clean the caboose—she almost missed the horse tied in front of her house.

*No saddle. I thought I was the only one in the Valley to sometimes ride bareback. Hmmm, except for Indians.* She opened the door into the house.

## Chapter Three

As she opened the door, the murmur of voices silenced. Luvella swallowed a small gasp. There, sitting at the kitchen table next to Mama, was an Indian. She searched Mama's face for signs of terror; there were none—just fatigue showing in her eyes. Mama put her hand on the sleeve of the man at her elbow. "Isaac, this is my youngest. Luvella, this is your great Uncle Isaac. He is married to your great Aunt Hilda—your grandma's sister."

The man stood and nodded. He was a tall man. Long black hair, streaked with ample strands of gray, framed his face, his dark eyes, and high cheekbones. *Oh Glory! That Indian is my uncle!*

"I am pleased to meet you, Uncle Isaac." She recovered from her rude reaction. She set her magazine on the hearth to read later and stood behind Mama, her hands on Mama's shoulders.

"Are you feeling all right, Mama? You look tired."

Mama put her hand over Luvella's and sighed. "I'm fine, Luvella. Aunt Hilda is very sick and needs help, probably for just a few days." She looked at Uncle Isaac, who was still standing and rotating the brim of his black hat through his hands.

He spoke with a clipped accent, his voice deep and resonant. "I shouldn't have come to you like this, Margaret. But she can't do anything for herself now, and before she fell into her deep sleep, she asked if I could get a woman to help her. She asked for you."

He sat again, once Luvella sat next to Mama. "I can't do much for her any more, but I surely would like to please her these last few days."

"Oh," Luvella said. "That sounds so…so sad. I'm very sorry. But Mama, you simply can't go now. Dr. Jordan said you have to rest."

"I know, honey." Mama looked at her hands, folded on the table, and then looked up at Luvella, her eyes begging. "I feel… It's been so long… Aunt Hilda never asked us for anything…" She stopped, shaking her head slowly.

Uncle Isaac shifted his feet under the table and cleared his throat.

Luvella sighed, understanding what her mother meant. Aunt Hilda had lived just across Muncy Creek when Mama was growing up. Mama would tell Luvella stories of how much fun Aunt Hilda had been at family picnics and holiday barn parties. But when Aunt Hilda married, she moved to Forksville and had hardly ever been mentioned in Mama's family since. When she was mentioned, it was always, "…you know, the one who married an Indian." White people just didn't do that.

But Luvella could hear the regret in Mama's voice and knew what Mama expected of her.

*Now is not the time, Mama!* she wanted to say, thinking of the caboose, the move, and how she had yet to tell her family. "I'll go in your place, Mama," Luvella said, swallowing the lump in her throat. "I really *have* to go to the merchants' meeting tomorrow first, though." She looked at Uncle Isaac. "What time do you want us to start in the morning?"

"If we don't have to take a wagon, we can cut across the mountain. Then it will only take…mebbe four, five hours, giving the horses time to rest. Can you ride?" He looked at Luvella, eying her lace-trimmed dress.

Luvella knew her small stature gave the impression of delicateness and femininity, so she forgave her great uncle this small mistake. "Of course," she said sweetly. "So, if we leave by eleven or noon tomorrow, we'll be there while it's still daylight?"

Uncle Isaac nodded, concern wrinkling his forehead. "If you can keep up, that would give us enough time. Hilda is being taken care of now by another grandniece, who is almost ready to give birth. It is not good for her to be with death when she is about to give new life."

Mama spoke up. "Uncle Isaac, Luvella is an excellent rider, but I hope you won't drive her too hard. She'll need her get-up-and-go to nurse Aunt Hilda."

"Don't worry, Mama. I'll be fine." Luvella rose from the table. "And now, I have to tell people of an earlier time for the business meeting tomorrow, so please excuse me, Uncle Isaac.

"Mama, I'll quick change and ride Daisy so I can be back in time to finish cooking dinner. That beef smells delicious." She grinned and patted her stomach. "Anything I'll need to get for my trip?"

When both Uncle Isaac and Mama shook their heads, she grabbed the *Harper's Magazine* and flew up the stairs to change into her riding skirt. No reading by the hearth tonight.

Later, she felt much braver galloping into the Valley to the train depot. Those men would never catch her, even if they were on horseback, too. She still kept an eye out for them, even as she raced through her mental list of what she had to do before she left for Forksville with Uncle Isaac: while she tells Mr. Johannson of the earlier meeting time, maybe she'll get approval to rent from the W and NB Railroad; stop at the store and ask Steckie to be early for tomorrow morning's meeting; and tell him she'll be away for a few days.

*Oh! How many days will I be away? Uncle Isaac never said.*

Daisy stopped at the pull on the reins. Luvella dismounted and tied the horse to the hitch in front of the depot. She slowed slightly to enter, remembering Mama's constant reminder to "act seemly, Luvella." She smiled when Mr. Johannson looked up.

"Your daddy won't let you take the caboose now, ain't that right, Luvella? Just after I received the railroad's acceptance?" Mr. Johannson frowned.

"No such thing, Mr. Johannson." Luvella's smile broadened upon hearing the good news. "I have to go to Forksville for a few days, and I'd like everything in place before I leave. So, the railroad has approved?" she asked, just so she could actually hear him say the words.

"Well-ll, yes it has, Luvella." He folded his arms in front of him. "You have your caboose to rent under the name of L. Andersson. They never even asked about the name. But right after that, another man came in here and said he'd like to *buy* the caboose." Mr. Johannson put one hand in his pants pocket. "But I don't know about that. He has to talk to the railroad. I mean, there's the car, and there's the land it's on." He pressed his lips together and frowned, rubbing his chin with his hand.

Luvella couldn't speak, as if all the air had gone from her lungs into the depot and pressed against her.

"I ain't really sure about this man—a stranger in town. Do you know him, Luvella? He sorta looks like a dandy—always too neat and he wears a derby." Mr. Johannson let out a small "Ha!" and shook his head.

Luvella turned away from him, struggling for breath, for strength. "I don't know who he is," she said softly, "but I know he seems to be making everyone in the Valley nervous. Steckie said he's coming to our meeting tomorrow."

The only sound in the depot was the click-click of the pendulum on the wall clock as the two stood, facing each other. Then a train whistle wailed in the distance, and Mr. Johannson pulled his watch from its pocket.

"The 5:44's coming," he said. "Right now, the railroad owns the caboose. I'll let you know if this dandy changes that."

Luvella pulled three coins from her pocket and gave them to Mr. Johannson, counting. "Five, six, seven—this is for my first month's rent." A ripple of satisfaction ran through her body at the look of surprise on his face. "Do you have a receipt handy? Just so we both have our records up to snuff."

While he went to his desk to write out the receipt, Luvella said, "I hope we can start our meeting tomorrow morning at nine o'clock exactly because I have to go to Forksville to help a very sick aunt. That's why I'm here now—to announce an earlier start—but I brought my rent money just to be prepared.

"Please don't mention this to anyone just yet, Mr. Johannson. I want to do this exactly right, and I read in the *Harper's Magazine* that timing is everything."

Mr. Johannson's laugh filled the small depot. "That magazine oughtta pay you a wage, Luvella, the way you read it and pass their information on to all of us."

Luvella pocketed the receipt from him and tried to contain the giggle that was climbing from her stomach. "Thank you, Mr. Johannson. I'll see you tomorrow at nine on the button." She was already out the door, stifling her giggle, which was dangerously close to tears. She ran across the road to Anna's hotel.

Mr. Smythe was sitting behind his desk with *that man*, and Luvella immediately straightened her face when he looked up at her, eyes as cold as the creek in winter. Mr. Smythe quickly nodded toward the same room she was in before, and Luvella knew that was where she'd find Anna.

She knocked on the door and closed it behind her before she snickered, her hands over her mouth to stifle the sounds. Anna knew and jumped up from her chair. "You did it! You got the caboose!" Luvella could only nod, the giggles bringing tears and a bear hug from Anna.

"I really have to get back to Mama." Luvella gulped air and wiped her eyes. "I have to tell Mama and Daddy tonight, but please don't tell anyone else just yet, Anna. I'm going to help Mama's sick aunt in Forksville for a few days, so I want to make sure I tell the right people at the right time. And this isn't the right time."

Anna nodded toward the door. "Did you see that awful man out there with my father? He scares me, Luvella, and he makes Daddy all quiet and jittery." Anna wiped her eyes as they filled with tears that followed paths down each cheek. "He's here all the time now. When he leaves, he comes back in less than half the hour."

She blew her nose gently into her handkerchief. "I feel like Mama, Daddy, and I are all in a prison." She began to sob. Luvella hugged her and patted her back. "And he's our jailer." Anna finished, the sobs working into quiet hysteria.

Luvella held Anna's shoulders, pushing her to arm's length and shaking her, very gently.

"You have to help your parents by being brave yourself. He makes everyone jittery, Anna," she said. "You know, he even told Mr. Johannson he wants to buy the caboose. Can you imagine?" Her mind raced. *How can he do that? What will he do with the caboose?* "When I get back from Forksville, we'll talk about what we can do about him. And Anna"—Luvella walked to the door and turned to face her friend—"we *will* do something about him. Now I really have to hurry. Oh! Anna," she whispered, "would you tell your father that our meeting will start early tomorrow? At nine. If *that man* doesn't know about the change of time, he just may miss a few things." She winked and Anna grinned.

Luvella opened the door to the inn's lobby. The man was still there with Mr. Smythe and the silhouette of him, standing over Mr. Smythe, refreshed an image in her head, gone almost before it was fully formed. But the image, that outline, had been clear enough for her to recognize it now. The caboose in her dream…the shadow of that man… It was the red headed stranger in their midst. *Even my dreams tell me he's evil.*

The release of her excitement and Anna's tears and the memory of her dream had sobered Luvella. *Good.*

*Now I can decide how to tell Mama and Daddy about the caboose and my move from Steckie's.* She led Daisy to the hitch in front of Steckie's store.

Inside, she ambled through the store, back to where Steckie stood behind his desk, and heaved her shoulders in a deep sigh. She remembered how Steckie and Bessie and Reeder had helped her set up her corner store. Even though her family was still recovering from typhoid, Daddy and Jake had come to the store her first day, just to see her in business. Her eyes brimmed. *They were still weak from pneumonia and came from their sick beds to show their respect for me and for what I was doing for our family.*

She stopped at the dippers and pails to blink her eyes dry. *And now I haven't even trusted them enough to tell them about my caboose.*

She took a deep breath as Steckie looked at her, questions written all over his face. "Well, Steckie, it's final. I just now settled the arrangement with the Williamsport and North Branch Railroad to rent the caboose." She managed a weak grin. "Next week it's mine!"

*No need to tell anyone else about that man wanting to buy the caboose. Mr. Johannson didn't seem to think much of the idea.*

"Next week," Steckie echoed. "That's pretty fast. But congratulations, Luvella. I don't know how you're going to fix that up, but if anyone can do it, you can." He looked over to her corner and around the store, and Luvella knew he was already deciding which of his merchandise would fill the void after she left.

"Another little problem came up, Steckie. Mama's Aunt Hilda is very sick and needs help. Uncle Isaac is home with Mama now, waiting to take me back to Forksville with him."

Steckie gaped. "Isn't your Aunt Hilda the one who…"

"Yes." Luvella nodded. "Uncle Isaac is an Indian. He seems nice, and Mama wants him to take me to Forksville. But we have to go tomorrow, which means I've changed our meeting to nine. We'll leave right after our merchants' meeting. Do you care if I ask Bessie to help you mind my store while I'm gone?"

"No, not at all, Luvella," he answered. "She can bring the baby right here with us. You do what you have to do for Mama and Aunt Hilda. And I think your new place of business will be a ringer."

Luvella grinned more easily now and warned Steckie about not telling anyone. On her way out, she noticed the tall stranger looking through the seeds, just inside the door. She hadn't heard him enter the store. *How long has he been there? How much did he hear?* She turned to look at Steckie, matching her frown with his, then swished out the door.

## Chapter Four

Luvella nudged Daisy with her knees and gave her free rein, the ride to Bessie's only a minute. After telling Bessie about the trip to Forksville and that Steckie had agreed to have her work at the store, Luvella warned, "Watch out for that tall red-haired man, Bessie. He's up to no good, that's a fact."

"Don't worry about the store, Luvella, *or* that man. I'll take care of *both,*" Bessie said with a chuckle. "But tell me about Aunt Hilda and Uncle Isaac. I've never seen him."

"Aunt Hilda is"—Luvella stopped, her hand resting on the doorknob—"she's dying and she's been asking Uncle Isaac for Mama to come see her."

"Oh, poor Aunt Hilda. Everyone used to say she was so beautiful, and headstrong, too." Bessie, who was eighteen years older than Luvella, remembered, looking into the distance. "Like you, Luvella." Bessie nudged her with an elbow.

"You, too." Luvella nudged Bessie back as she opened the door. They grinned together.

"What's Uncle Isaac like?" Bessie asked.

Luvella pushed the door almost closed and thought a second. "Well, he's an Indian; there's no mistaking that, Bessie. He's very gentlemanly, and I think he's…wise. I don't know why I think that, but, well, he's very quiet and his eyes," she hesitated, looking into the distance, "just seem to understand." Luvella pushed the door open again. "I like him, and I'll know him better after our trip." She hugged Bessie goodbye. "I really have to hurry."

When she arrived home, about five minutes later, Luvella turned Daisy loose in the pasture. On her way to the house, she noticed Uncle Isaac's horse. It was large—about fifteen hands—mostly dark brown with white markings. It stood quietly at the hitching post. Luvella spoke to him. "They must have forgotten you were out here." She stroked his mane.

"I'll get you more comfortable, poor thing." Then she led Uncle Isaac's horse to the pasture, too. *Let him get used to the place before we bed him down.* She unbridled him and rubbed his nose to calm him. He shifted legs, relaxed, and bent his head for another nose pat. For a few minutes, she watched the two horses to see if they would tolerate each other. Although they stayed at opposite ends of the paddock, it appeared that the distance they kept from each other was a friendly one.

In the house, Luvella told Uncle Isaac about moving his horse, and he thanked her. He shook his head slowly and frowned. "I forgot about Kitschi," he said, pronouncing it Kee-chee.

Mama sighed. "That's because you're thinking about Aunt Hilda."

Luvella stood at the table and looked at both Mama and Uncle Isaac. *I* have *to get this done.* She inhaled sharply and forced a broad smile. "Mama, I have the best news! Maybe it will help you feel a little better, especially after hearing about Aunt Hilda." She softened her smile, out of respect for Aunt Hilda's serious condition.

"I've been talking to Mr. Johannson recently (she should say 'for some weeks now', she thought) about renting that old caboose for my store, my very own store." She placed her hands on either side of her mouth, then lowered them and folded them together. "He just now told me the W and NB Railroad has approved the arrangement, and I can start moving in next week. I've already paid him my first month's rent." She smiled, looking first at Mama and then Uncle Isaac, and sat next to her mother.

Mama put a hand to her forehead as if this news pained her. "You mean, you did all this without telling us or talking to your father about it?" Mama looked quickly at Uncle Isaac and then back at Luvella. Uncle Isaac shifted in his seat at Mama's distress and rose from his chair.

"I'll check on the horses," he said softly, his voice sounding like satin-smooth paddles slipping into deep water.

"Mama," Luvella hastened to explain. "Both you and Daddy agree I run a very respectable business for a woman. You've been sick, too, and worrying wouldn't be good for you. I knew you both would worry about me trying to bite off more than I could chew, so I just didn't say anything."

"I'm worrying now, Luvella." Mama looked at her, and Luvella almost cried. Mama's face was red, she had tears in her eyes, and the hand, still on her forehead, trembled slightly.

"Oh Mama. I'm sorry. I was trying to help you get well—not make you worse." She put her arm around Mama's shoulders. "Let's talk more later. I think you've overdone today. If you go to bed now, you can rest until dinner."

"I'm not going to bed in the middle of the day." Mama's hand fell to the table in front of her. "But I will sit in my rocking chair and just close my eyes for a few minutes. I don't know what your daddy will say when you tell him about this caboose idea." Half grunting and half sighing as she stood, Mama hobbled to her rocking chair, which was facing the fireplace even though there was no fire there. She sank into her chair and immediately rested her head against its back and closed her eyes.

Luvella stood at the table and watched her. *Poor Mama. She's feeling poorly, and all these things are comin' down the road at her—all at the same time. I should have waited to tell her about the caboose, but then…I think that would have hurt her more.*

Luvella turned, stepping into the kitchen area, and pulled a large kettle from the cupboard. Standing on her tiptoes at the sink, she pumped water into the kettle. She carried it over to the large iron stove and set it on the medium-sized burner plate. She opened the stove door under the burner plate to stoke the fire in the chamber, added a small log, and closed the door. While the kettle of water was heating, she pared the potatoes and carrots for dinner.

*I'll get the vegetables cooking, set the table, and be outside to tell Daddy before he comes in from the sawmill.* She salted the water in the kettle, put the vegetables in, and rushed between cupboard and table to place the dishes and silverware around.

She glanced toward the rocking chair. Mama's head was leaning back, stretching her neck, and her mouth was relaxed into a slightly open position. Luvella closed the door softly behind her and rushed to feed Daisy and settle her in. She showed Uncle Isaac where to bed down Kitschi and filled a bucket of oats for him as well. *Was that the approaching drum of horses' hooves or her heart pounding in her throat?* She looked toward the road. Daddy, Bill, Jake and Reeder were home.

Uncle Isaac moved into the shadows of Kitschi's stall. *This must be sorely awful for him, to ask Aunt Hilda's family for help after all these years of...what? Distance? No, it was much more than that.*

"Uncle Isaac," she called to him. "Could you help me?"

He stepped into a beam of late sunlight winking through the open barn door. Only his eyes were smiling. "The young lady who can ride a horse sees a mighty hurdle ahead?"

Luvella hung her head and nodded. "Would you busy my brothers so I can talk to Daddy alone for a minute?" She looked up at his face, a map of wrinkles around glittering brown eyes and a slightly hooked nose. His mouth, lips full and smooth within the wrinkled mass, was smiling at her.

"A wise girl would make him chief again, Luvella." He nodded toward Daddy, patted Kitschi's withers, and emerged from the stall. "I will entertain the young warriors."

Luvella watched him walk slowly through the open barn doors and reach for the bit on Charlie, the wagon horse nearest him. Jake, driving the wagon, called "Whoa!" and pulled the brake handle against the wagon wheel. Luvella rushed forward.

"Daddy, Jake, this is Uncle Isaac, Aunt Hilda's husband. Uncle Isaac, this is Daddy and Jake, my oldest brother, is driving. Bill, he's next oldest, is in the back of the wagon with Reeder." She pointed to each person in turn. "Reeder's only a year older than me." Daddy was the first to jump down and shake Uncle Isaac's hand, followed by Jake, Bill, and finally Reeder.

"I'm a year and a half older," Reeder corrected, his brown-black eyes glaring at her.

"Aunt Hilda's doing poorly, and I'm going to go back with Uncle Isaac to help her through her last days." There was immediate silence until Daddy looked up. "I'm truly sorry, Isaac. We'll help any which way."

"Thank you, Will," Uncle Isaac said. "I'd appreciate your looking over Luvella's horse for our trip tomorrow. I'll help the boys with these horses and the wagon."

Daddy looked puzzled at first, then followed Luvella as she walked toward Daisy's stall. "We're going to ride over the mountain to Forksville. Leave right after our meeting tomorrow." She opened the stall door and went in, feeling the hay on the floor swirl around her feet and release its pungent scent. "Are her shoes in good shape, you think?"

Daddy pulled a lantern off a hook on the barn wall. He took a match from the match tray under the lantern, struck it against his pants, and lit the wick in the lantern. He knelt on the stall floor with the lantern and examined each hoof. Luvella kept swallowing the saliva that rushed into her mouth.

"Uh, Daddy?" He finished with the inspection, stood, and looked at her.

"The hooves are all fine, Luvella. I just had them

shod a coupla weeks ago."

"Daddy?" Luvella stood between him and the stall door. "I'd like to tell you something. Something important."

He held the lantern up to see her face, his own lined with fatigue, sawdust sprinkling his mustache. "Ayup, Luvella? What is it?"

She told him, slowly, as clearly as she could so it would be over. At the end, she added, "Would you tell the family at dinner time? And ask them to please not tell anyone until I'm ready?"

He blew out the lantern light, but not before Luvella saw his eyes, tired and sad. "This is done, Luvella? Done?"

She whispered back. "Yes, Daddy. I went to Mr. Johannson today and paid him seven dollars for the month's rent."

He exhaled a deep, trembling sigh and put his arm around Luvella's shoulders, leading her out of the barn and toward the house. "A man gets the fever and his daughter takes off like a herd of buffalo." He shook his head. "Luvella, I won't hold you back—you've proved that you have a head for business. But I've run the sawmill for ten years, and I could help you with important decisions. I would like you to let me help you in the future—before you make any big changes."

"I will, Daddy. I promise." Her heart sang. But remembering Mr. Johannson's words "…he wants to buy the caboose…" sobered her immediately:

"I may need you soon," she said. "Have you noticed that stranger in town? He wears a derby all the time."

Daddy stopped and faced her. "Ayep. I saw him

once, and I hear tell he's agitatin' Ben Smythe." He squinted at Luvella. "What about him?"

While Daddy pulled at his mustache, Luvella told him what Mr. Johannson had said. "Mr. Johannson acted like he didn't like the man, either, and said the railroad would have to approve selling it."

Daddy nodded as he thought. "I think we'd better have a lawful lease for you, Luvella, signed by the railroad and you. I'll talk to Lars about that," Daddy mused. "And we'll keep an eye on that fella with the derby."

Daddy turned toward the barn door. "Isaac, let's you and I go into the house. The boys can finish with the horses."

Inside, Luvella checked the food as Daddy, Uncle Isaac, and then her brothers washed up at the sink. Mama awoke from the clatter of boots and pumping water, and rose to light the lanterns and slice the bread for dinner.

Luvella ran out to the springhouse to bring in the cold milk and butter. She lifted the hook latch on its door and bent over to step inside. Her arms were too short to just reach in the dark recesses for their cold food. Leaving one foot behind her to keep the door from closing, she let her eyes adjust to the dark. Mountain rock formed the back of the dollhouse-sized structure and water trickling down it sounded like rain on the water barrel. Plink, plink… That constant drip of cold water helped keep the springhouse cold, even in the summer. She found the milk jug and butter pot and backed out.

In the house, she placed the beef roast on a platter and sliced it; she browned the meat juices for gravy while she drained the vegetables and put them—potatoes, carrots, and onions—all in one large bowl. As the men dried their faces and hands and came to the table, Luvella and Mama set the food out and sat for grace.

During dinner, Daddy and Uncle Isaac talked about President Taft "doing away with" Standard Oil Company, and their mill work, since Uncle Isaac worked for the lumber mill in Forksville. Then Isaac told how Aunt Hilda had wanted to see Mama.

Mama chuckled and everyone looked at her. Smiling, she said, "I remember when I was little, I made this clothespin doll and wrapped an old scrap of my mama's material around it for a dress. It was the ugliest thing you ever saw, but I was proud of it and gave it to Aunt Hilda. She made such a fuss over that doll." She wiped her forehead and clamped her lips together to stop their trembling.

"Years of foolishness," Daddy said, shaking his head. Uncle Isaac looked at him, but remained quiet. "Has it been tough for you, Isaac? And for Hilda?"

An awkward silence hung in the dinner air. Uncle Isaac slid his feet back and forth under the table and put his fork down. "At first." It was almost a whisper. He cleared his throat and then spoke more clearly. "When I was able to find work, it helped. Hilda was alone in the town for many years. The other women didn't invite her to the quilting parties or teas, or even conversation at the general store." He picked up his fork again and thrust it into a carrot. "But there are a few other Muncees who live near Forksville, and they welcomed Hilda. We built a cabin closer to them. My sister lives just outside of Forksville also, so we have been close to her and her family. Her grandson, Luke, is home from boarding school. They released him so he could be with his family and with Hilda."

Mama smiled. "Your sister's children must be doing good to afford a boarding school for their son."

Uncle Isaac snorted softly. "It's Carlisle Industrial, paid for and run by the government, and Luke didn't have a choice at first. After Wounded Knee and the relocation of so many of my people, the government took all our children of the ones who settled in Pennsylvania and New York, and the ones out West, too. The government put them in boarding schools far from home so they couldn't run away, to learn the white man's ways, to wear white man's clothes, to learn white man's language."

Uncle Isaac didn't smile. "The government doesn't want Indian children to be home where they can learn our people's ways. In fact, under law, we are forbidden to practice our traditions."

Luvella stopped eating and stared at Uncle Isaac. "But that's horrible! How old is poor little Luke?"

This time Uncle Isaac smiled. "Poor little Luke is eighteen and almost as tall as I am—a true Muncee." Luvella blushed, but she could see the pride in Uncle Isaac's face. "He was allowed to come home before the end of the school year—and before football practice—for Hilda's funeral ceremony and will not return there. He has long finished his government schooling, has assisted the doctor in their infirmary the past year while playing and practicing football for Carlisle, and now that he's home, we have already started his Muncee training, secretly, of course."

He picked up his coffee mug. "That, by the way, is

not to be mentioned again, please." He sipped his coffee. "I shouldn't have said anything, but you're family."

Daddy arranged his fork and knife on his plate, cleared of his food. "You have our word on that, Isaac." He rubbed the stubble on his chin and added, "Luvella, would you like to pour the coffee now? Speaking of our children, I have something I want to brag about."

Luvella bounced from her chair, grabbed the coffeepot with a potholder, and filled the mugs around the table. She could feel Mama watching her. When she sat in her place, Daddy lifted his mug for a sip of the steaming brew while everyone at the table sat at attention.

"Pretty soon, this here little girl," he said, pointing to Luvella, "will be doing her store business in that old caboose next to the depot. And I expect she's going to need some help moving everything from Steckie's." He looked around the table, his eyebrows raised in a questioning mode. "And what about getting the caboose cleaned out first?" he asked Luvella, who nodded yes.

"Hoo, Luvella! Good for you!" Jake said. "I'll help you do anything you need done." Bill and Reeder agreed. Mama smiled at Luvella but didn't say anything.

Her father spoke up again. "Luvella doesn't want people to know yet. It's part of her advertising plan, I think." He grinned, his mustache spreading across his face. "So keep that news inside this house for now, too."

Mama rose from her place with new energy born of relief. "I knew there was a reason I wanted to bake a rhubarb pie this morning. I must've had an inkling of a celebration in the air."

The chorus of male voices saying "Oh" and "Ah" made Mama and Luvella laugh. Uncle Isaac winked at Luvella as she passed his plate of pie to him and, grinning, she mouthed "Thank you" to him.

"Daddy." Luvella continued passing out the plates of pie. "There's an old stove in the caboose for colder weather, and Mr. Johannson told me before that it still works. But today, we found two jugs of moonshine hidden in it."

Everyone stopped, forks in mid-air.

"Moonshine." Mama's face went white. There was no hard stuff allowed in her house.

Jake pointed his fork at Daddy. "Tell you what. Why don't Reeder and Bill and I walk up to the tavern tonight and see what those men are saying? If one or more of them aren't sneaking into the caboose at night, I'll bet they know who is."

Daddy nodded. "But be careful."

"And no shenanigans." Mama frowned, and they all knew she'd better not smell spirits on them when they came home.

After everyone finished dessert and got up from the table, Mama said, "All right, Luvella, I'll help you redd the table. And I'll dry the dishes tonight—you wash them while I sit a bit. You've got a big day tomorrow."

Grateful for the reprieve, Luvella jumped into her chore. The men went out onto the porch, the evening gathering place when it was warm. Her brothers continued off to the tavern. Luvella heard Daddy's and Uncle Isaac's voices when they became animated: "Germany threatening England and France…" and "Hardly any more malaria at Panama Canal…" Their easy conversation was separated by long silences. Twilight time, Mama always called it. As soon as she could, Luvella lit a lantern and rushed up the stairs to her room and her copy of *Harper's*.

Her bedroom, located in the back corner of the house, had two windows. One overlooked the back section of the side yard and the other offered a beautiful view of the back yard and the creek. Both windows looked out to North Mountain. Luvella's bed, which she used to share with Bessie, was nudged into the opposite corner of the room.

"Finally," she whispered, dropping onto the side of the bed, and read the Table of Contents. Two articles piqued her interest, but she thought she had time for only one. She chose "Ballyhoo Your Advertising!" and began to scan through it. Halfway down the first column, she pinched her eyebrows together and sat closer to the lantern. "Start at the beginning, Luvella."

Carefully, she read the entire article. Once finished, she blinked her eyes as they peered into nothingness. She dropped her head then and stared at the open magazine, thinking, thinking.

A framed informational insert at the bottom corner caught her eye. After scanning its text, she took extra care to re-read the facts. She dropped the magazine and paced.

"Oh my!" She stopped pacing abruptly, like a cat pouncing on its prey, and realization trickled over her. She laughed and shouted, "Oh Glory!" She heard the silence from downstairs and ran to the top of the stairs. Only Mama's eyes stared up at her, but the wisps of pipe smoke wafting through the screen door told her Daddy was nearby.

"Daddy! Mama!" She bounded down the stairs. "*Harper's* just gave me the perfect answer to Muncy Valley's problems. Wait'll I tell you!"

## Chapter Five

Mama sat in her rocking chair on her side of the fireplace and stared at Luvella, who stood with her back toward the darkened fire pit and faced the large combined dining room/parlor. Daddy wandered in from the porch, followed by Uncle Isaac, all looking at Luvella.

"The new *Harper's* has this article about, well, it's about advertising and marketing—about a festival—for a big neighborhood, and we could do the same thing for our whole town." She looked from one to the other but settled her gaze on Daddy. She raised her left hand to tuck her hair behind her ear.

"Did someone actually try this out yet, Luvella?" Daddy asked, like a teacher questioning a student she's sure knows the answer.

"Oh yes." Luvella moved forward, her father and Isaac parting to make an aisle for her. Back and forth, between fireplace and dining table she walked, clenching her hands together, frowning and then smiling broadly when a new idea struck her. "In Brooklyn—that's a part of New York City that's like a city all by itself—the merchants were trying to get more people to come to them and to buy their products."

Her head bent, her fingers steepled and pressed against her mouth, she stopped and grinned. "Oh, Daddy. This could be so perfect for Muncy Valley. I keep thinking of other little things we can do to make it successful."

"Just tell me what it's all about. Please, Luvella." He tapped his pipe against the side of the fireplace. The burnt ashes fell into the pit.

"Yes," she said. "Well, those Brooklyn merchants planned a big festival, like a big holiday celebration, except it wasn't a holiday. They had it right on the boardwalks in front of their stores and even into some sections of the road. All the businesses took part and marked some of their items down—on sale, and got other special products in just for the festival. They had food and music and dancing and everything."

She took two steps again and turned back toward Mama and Daddy. "They said the festival was not only very successful, but people are coming back to their stores. They made new customers. And it was so popular and unusual, *Harper's Magazine* even wrote this story about it.

"Daddy, I want to put it to the members at our meeting tomorrow. Steckie usually ends up letting me run it anyway, especially when I have a new idea for the group. We could have our own festival. We could all put certain products on sale to draw people into our stores. We could have Mr. Johannson and Mr. Pearson play their fiddles right down there by the depot and the inn." She stopped and twirled around.

"The inn!" she shrieked. "That could help Mr. Smythe's inn, too." She stood perfectly still, thinking. "And the farrier. Just think. Every single business owner would profit from a festival."

Uncle Isaac's bass tones slipped into the conversation. "Luvella, many Muncee women around

Forksville make beautiful baskets—all kinds, all sizes, all colors. I could collect a big supply and bring them down for you to sell." He thought a minute and smiled. "I could bring you enough baskets for a small supply in every store."

Luvella looked up at him, staring blankly. No one spoke. Just as Uncle Isaac started to back away, Luvella whispered, "That's our festival." She pushed her hands into the air above her and brought them down, pressing her hair back, laughing giddily. "We'll have a *Basket Bonanza*. Baskets in every single store or business. Each business will display some small items for sale in some baskets and then display the baskets themselves for sale. We can have baked food sales, a big picnic down by the inn, right where the music is, and some of the women can sell some baskets with a picnic lunch in them already."

She stopped, turned slowly to look at her father, and let out a long sigh, like the last steam bellow of a halting locomotive. "Daddy?"

Daddy was tapping his lips with the stem of an unlit pipe. He pointed the stem in the direction of Luvella, nodding thoughtfully. "I s'pose even the lumber mill could be part of the hoopla. We could sell toothpicks and firewood—and baskets." He looked at Uncle Isaac, and they both laughed. "Luvella, you bring it up at the meeting, and I'll be right behind you." He started to get up from the chair. "It's a real dandy idea."

Luvella glided closer to her father. "Um, Daddy. There's one more thing." He sat back down.

Mama rolled her eyes and leaned her head onto her hand, her elbow resting on the arm of her chair. "Luvella, you plumb exhaust me."

Daddy and Uncle Isaac snickered.

"It's hard to keep apace with her." Daddy agreed. He reached over to tug at a ringlet falling on his daughter's shoulder and smiled.

Luvella knelt on the floor next to Daddy and put her hands on the arm of his chair. She loved the sweet smell of the Prince Albert tobacco coming from the pouch in his shirt pocket. "There's a notice in the magazine of an October conference of the chamber of commerce in Pittsburgh. It sounds like they have a group just like ours, all business owners, all working together to make their businesses grow, but they call it a chamber of commerce. Lots of towns in Pennsylvania have a…a chamber, and they're all invited to this conference. We should name our group"—she looked up and held her hands as if they were holding a sign—"The Muncy Valley Chamber of Commerce. Daddy, I want to go to that meeting. I have to go."

He closed his eyes and leaned his head against the back of the chair. "Luvella, that's too much." He was rolling his head back and forth.

Mama spoke. "Luvella. You're a young lady. You can't go traipsing around the country all by yourself. And, 'sides, that chamber or whatever they call themselves won't let a girl in fer love nor money."

Luvella was prepared for these objections. "Mama, I know you don't like the suffragists, but they've forced a lot of changes. I already told you about women working in offices on those typing machines. And women can go to a lot of other places now, too.

"I wouldn't speak up at the conference. I'd just listen to see how their groups work. Just think, Daddy, how much that would help our Valley."

Silence fell on the room like a heavy snowfall. Momentarily, Mama set to rocking, much too fast for a sickly woman, and the squeak of her chair pierced the group's deliberation.

"And how would you pay for this trip? It would be at least one overnight." Daddy looked straight ahead.

Luvella breathed more evenly. *He's considering it.* "Either we take it out of the group's bank account, or each member of the group would pay toward the cost of the trip. I would be representing the group, not just myself."

Daddy nodded slightly, his pipe tapping his mouth again. "Why not send Lars Johannson or Pieter Pearson? They're both good men."

Luvella stood, slapping the arm of her father's chair. "But I'm the one who started our group; I'm the one who organizes everything and practically runs the meetings; and I'm the one with all the ideas." She started pacing again.

"Daddy, they're good businessmen right here in Muncy Valley, but they really aren't good at finding new ways to sell or even of knowing a good idea when they first see it." She twirled to face him once more. "They have to be talked into every new thing."

"Try to be patient. These men, and I'm one of them, didn't have eight years of schoolin' like you did. We've all learned by doin'. So, just let me think on that one. I've gotta be talked into it, too." Daddy got up from his chair, ending the discussion, and went out on the porch to light his pipe. Mama had forbade him to smoke in the house.

For an awkward instant, there was complete silence. Then, everyone moved at once, Uncle Isaac toward the porch, Luvella for bed. She leaned over to kiss Mama's forehead. "'Night, Mama. I'm going to get ready for the trip tomorrow—and for the meeting." Turning to Uncle Isaac, she said, "I'll try real hard to be back home and ready to start by ten thirty tomorrow. Is that all right?"

He was still nodding when she started up the stairs. Once in her room, she went directly to the window facing the northern tip of North Mountain, pushed the window up as high as it would go, and leaned out with her elbows on the sill. She could smell the rain, although there was none yet. The wind had died, and the expectant stillness in the air was a sure sign a summer storm was almost here.

She looked out and up at her mountain. Everything was black outside; there was no real view, no nodding of pine branches or chirps of robins in her support. "You're a big help," she said to the unresponsive blackness. The moon silhouetted the clouds, quietly assembling. Luvella scanned them and knew they were preparing for a showdown.

"Fits my mood just dandy," she said, smiling. "I love storms. Everything is clean afterward. You have yours tonight, and I'll have mine tomorrow morning."

## Chapter Six

Luvella, riding on the wagon bench with her father, looked over her notes for the meeting and thought about what she would say about the trip to Pittsburgh. Daddy still hadn't said another word about it. She was sure all the members would like the festival idea—especially Mr. Smythe. And he'd bring the other men to agree. But the chamber of commerce…

The merchants' group membership had grown from the original five members—Steckie, Daddy, Mr. Johannson, Mr. Smythe, and Luvella—to every business owner in the Valley. Jude Harley, the banker, was the eleventh and newest member, and now the meetings were held in the church so everyone could fit comfortably.

Luvella entered the church and walked toward the front from where Steckie and she would speak. She was halfway down the aisle when she noticed the red hair, the tall man sitting right in the front row of benches.

*Oh! Wouldn't you know he'd sit right up front.* She hesitated, then turned to see if Daddy was behind her. But he was tethering the horses. She scanned the church again. Mr. Smythe was sitting next to the stranger and on the other side of the aisle were Mr. Johannson and Mr. Pearson. *That's good.* She headed directly for Mr. Pearson.

"Would you save the place next to you for my

father, please?" She wanted to go over to Mr. Smythe and say, "Mr. Smythe, this meeting is for members only," but she didn't. She just looked at him and then at the stranger.

Mr. Smythe blushed and cleared his throat, but before he could speak, the red-haired man stood and looked down at Luvella. "I'm the new owner of the inn and, as such, am a member of this group." He smiled beneath cold blue eyes. "My name is Sigfried Bocke."

Luvella raised her eyebrows and looked at Mr. Smythe. He said, "It isn't finalized yet, Luvella, but Mr. Bocke is very interested in purchasing the inn."

*Just what I wanted to hear. But does that mean Mr. Bocke has changed his mind and now only wants to buy my caboose?* She turned away, as if to push that thought behind her, along with Mr. Bocke. *Mr. Johannson acted like Mr. Bocke's purchase of the caboose was not going to be accepted by the railroad, so I don't think I have to worry. Oh, how Mr. Smythe will love what I have to say today. But how will I deal with our Mr. Bocke if he tries to take over here?*

Steckie was still at the church door, so Luvella went back and repeated to him Mr. Bocke's and Mr. Smythe's statements. Then she returned to the front to prepare for when she would speak. She arranged her notes on the lectern—twice, as a matter of fact. Daddy came to the front at Mr. Pearson's beckon and sat next to him. Luvella's father watched her as she meticulously tidied her papers, probably wondering what was going on. He always told her he dreaded what was coming next when she was thinking hard.

She looked up and scanned the people assembled. As she sat next to her father, Steckie went to the lectern to begin the meeting. He cleared his throat and spoke up over the quiet conversations. "It looks like everyone is here," Steckie said, "and as you all know, Luvella has to leave on a trip today. So let's start."

The rustle of clothing and scuff of boots on the floor quieted as the folks settled into attention.

"Pieter, could you begin by giving us a report on our money?" Steckie stood aside so Mr. Pearson could come up front.

Pieter Pearson ambled forward from his front seat and stood next to Steckie. His tall frame, with his thick blond hair, bushy eyebrows, and sandy mustache, were counterpoints to Steckie's medium build and dark, curly hair.

"We have twenty dollars and fifteen cents sitting in Jude's bank, now that he's a member." He grinned at Mr. Harley, and several of the men chuckled. "There are still some dues outstanding for this year. You know who you are." Luvella felt, rather than saw, Mr. Smythe wriggle in his seat. "We have no debts," Mr. Pearson finished and went back to his seat next to Daddy.

"Thank you, Pieter." Steckie nodded at him. Then he faced the red-haired man. In crisp tones, he said, "Ben, would you introduce our guest for today?" He accented the word guest, and if the membership missed it, Luvella noted by his frown that Mr. Bocke did not. Steckie licked his lips in satisfaction.

Mr. Smythe stood and turned to the people. His shoulders sloped, his face drawn. "This here is Sigfried Bocke. He's lookin' to buy my inn and wants to see how our Valley businesses work together." Mr. Smythe turned to sit, and Mr. Bocke began to rise. Before he could stand and speak, Steckie raised his voice slightly over the murmured reactions to the inn news. "Thank you, Ben, and good luck to you. Now let's get to some new business Luvella wants to talk to us about."

Mr. Bocke settled back on his bench. Luvella could sense the glacial penetration of his eyes as she stepped up to the lectern and focused on the other people before her.

"I read an article in the new *Harper's* about how a group of business people in Brooklyn organized a festival."

Faces stared at her, alert, waiting. Even Mr. Bocke's eyes shifted to…curiosity? She explained the festival and its results. More staring. *They have no idea how we can use a festival.* Luvella wasn't surprised.

"First order of new business today." She glanced at Daddy when she said first. He didn't flinch. "I propose that Muncy Valley have a festival." The red head stiffened in his seat, his back pitch-fork straight. People looked at each other and back at Luvella. Shoes shuffled. "This is exactly what I suggest."

She laid out her plans: Every merchant participates; sale prices on a few items; others at full price; use the older children to help out; arrange some items on the porches of the stores, so the whole Main Street looks like a festival; music and dancing in front of the inn. At this point, Luvella looked at Mr. Smythe. He had already brightened, but at the thought of activity right in front of the inn, his shoulders squared and his back straightened.

Luvella continued, "If Mr. Johannson and Mr. Pearson would agree to fiddle for us, if we decorated the whole stores area of the Valley and be sure to use bright colors, and if we had a large picnic area right next to the music…" She smiled as everyone nodded and whispered to each other, and grins grew. She held her hand up to quiet them, never finishing her sentence.

"I recently learned of a source of baskets—handmade baskets. All sizes and colors and reasonably priced. I think baskets would make a good theme for the festival. Each place of business would have baskets, some to display their smaller items for sale and others to sell separately. I suggest we call the festival A Basket Bonanza." She realized she had never asked Uncle Isaac about prices of the baskets. After only a breath's hesitation, she added, "I'll get the exact price schedule soon. Another idea for using the baskets is to fill them with lunches or pies and sell the two as a package."

Mr. Smythe spoke up, a renewed vibrant timbre to his voice. "Luvella, that is a Jim-Dandy proposal. That will bring just what we need to Muncy Valley."

Luvella knew he meant just what I need for the inn. There were ayups and yups and heads bobbing. She continued, "Mr. Melk, you realize this will include you, too." The sandy-haired farrier, with arms and hands almost the size of a black bear's, beamed his relief.

Mr. Bocke's carrot-colored head swung around, first one way and then the other. His frown was deep, his movements agitated.

Luvella moved with the momentum. "Mr. Johannson, would you work with whoever you want to set up the music and dancing? Mr. Smythe, would you arrange for a picnic area? And could you make space in your inn in case of rain?" Luvella clenched her stomach muscles to keep from laughing. Mr. Smythe was almost bouncing off his bench with joy, and the red head was twisting within himself, his face crimson with anger.

"Mrs. Maarten, would you mind being in charge of the picnic baskets and the food? You can work with Mr. Smythe on the food. Umm, we may have to check with the new Food and Drug Administration on that now. I'll write them and find out.

"And finally, I will have a meeting very soon with you three so we can go over everything we've learned and decided. We have to move fast on this because we want to have the festival before the cold weather sets in. I'd say we should have it on the first Saturday in September." She looked around the church. No one said no.

Luvella shifted her papers in front of her. "The next order of business..." She glanced over at her father. *He was nodding.*

Her father stood, first looked at Luvella, and then turned to face the people. "I'll take this." Luvella held her breath. "Luvella discovered something else in *Harper's* magazine. It looks like there are other organizations, just like ours, in Pittsburgh and other big cities. Each city calls its group the chamber of commerce, and there is a convention of all the Pennsylvania Chambers in Pittsburgh this October."

Luvella eyed the people, simple folk, hard-working, mind-your-own-business people. A convention was big-city stuff and didn't concern them. They turned their puzzled faces to Willem Andersson.

Her father ran his hand over his graying hair. Luvella knew he was "working up a head of steam," as he called it. His voice rose, and he looked around, meeting each person eye-to-eye. "You're all my friends. You know I'm not a braggin' man." Assenting nods all around. "But Luvella here has done a good job in her own business and for all the businesses here in the Valley."

Mr. Smythe clapped his hands, big, slow claps. Mrs. Maarten took it up, and soon the church was filled with applause and a chorus of "ayups." Luvella bent her head, feeling the heat and the blush start in her face and travel clear to her toes. She blinked hard to clear her eyes of welling tears.

Her father continued. "Well, Luvella thinks it would be a big benefit to our businesses if we sent one of us, at the group's expense, to that convention." He shifted his weight from one foot to the other. "And I agree with her."

Mr. Sigfried Bocke leaped up from the front bench and spun around to face the people. "This is preposterous." Spittle sprayed from his mouth, like venom. "You're letting a frilly little girl lead you all by your noses."

Luvella's father, who stood only as high as Mr. Bocke's shoulder, almost crouched, as a bobcat does just before he lunges for the kill. He blurted loudly to be heard over the commotion, "Mr. Bocke, you are a guest here only. Please sit down."

The red head waved his arm, pointing at Luvella. "I suppose she's the one who wants to go to Pittsburgh and come back and tell you all what to do next."

Daddy, who was still standing in front on the other side of the aisle, said, "I am offering to go for the group. I think Luvella ought to go, too, because she has more business sense than the rest of us put together." Ayup…ayup…ayup. "And Mr. Bocke, my frilly little daughter's father told you to sit down." Daddy, his lumberjack biceps flexing under his shirt, glared the red head into his seat.

"Thank you, Daddy." Luvella bent her head in her father's direction. She explained further the chamber of commerce, its goals and its supporting and connecting branches around the country. She stood as tall as she could, then, and said, "I'd like to bring this to a vote today. We have to make reservations for their conference. How many want my father and me to go to Pittsburgh to see what other towns are doing to improve their business conditions?"

Mr. Harley raised his hand slowly, his face turning crimson when everyone looked at him. "How much will this trip cost?" he asked.

Mr. Johansson stood immediately. "I can answer that. Two round trip tickets on the W and NB to Pittsburgh, one night at an inn, would cost about five dollars." He nodded toward Luvella's father. "I expect you'd take care of your own meals?"

Both Daddy and Luvella said, "Yes," and Luvella repeated, "How many vote for the trip to the convention?"

Mr. Smythe immediately shot his hand up; Mr. Johannson looked around and slowly raised his hand. Mrs. Maarten and Mrs. Kiergen, sitting next to each other, raised their hands in unison, and the others all followed. Luvella noticed Mr. Harley was the last to agree. *But he's happy to take my money every week,* she complained to herself.

"Good. We're all together. The next step is to agree on paying the expenses. Everyone who agrees to that, raise your hand, please." This was quicker, since Mr. Johannson's casual estimate.

"Good." Luvella gathered her papers. "Mr. Johannson, Mr. Smythe, and Mrs. Maartens, please get your people together right now so you can begin festival plans immediately. I'll give you exact requests for money for Pittsburgh as soon as I know the details. Right now, let's start our festival plans while we're all here. Thank you everyone. The meeting is over."

Mr. Smythe ran to Luvella and grabbed her arm. "The Basket Bonanza is a lifesaver. That is exactly the…the spark we need to fire up Muncy Valley." He blushed at his own unintended eloquence. "Bless you, Luvella." He squeezed her arm and turned toward the people.

Mr. Bocke stood, looking abandoned and confused. Then he sidled next to Luvella and hissed in her ear, "You'll regret this, you…you little ninny." He whirled around and slithered out of the church.

Daddy came to the front. "Come on, Luvella. I'll take you back to the house." He winked at her, and his mustache broadened over a wide smile.

Just before he pulled the horses into their drive, he said, "Oh, by the by, Luvella. I slipped my Colt .45 into your saddlebag this morning. It's loaded, so be careful with that bag. I know you're a crack shot, but remember, aim just a mite high when you shoot with that gun." He waited while she jumped down from the wagon. "Don't ever go into those woods without protection. Especially at night."

# Chapter Seven

Uncle Isaac stood near the barn door, holding the bridles of both horses. He had saddled Luvella's Daisy for the long trip and waited, quietly talking to the horses. Luvella quickly changed into a riding skirt, the closest thing to pants Mama would let her wear, and grabbed her saddle bag carefully. *If Mama finds out I have a gun in here, both Daddy and I will be in trouble.* Mama stood by the door to the kitchen and handed their lunches, wrapped in a cloth, to Luvella as she raced to the doorway.

"Goodbye, Mama. You get your rest, now." They hugged each other.

"Luvella," Mama whispered. "Explain to Aunt Hilda why I'm not there with her." Mama choked through the words. "And tell her…tell her I…I've missed her terribly all these years." She waved to Uncle Isaac, hugged her daughter again, and turned to enter the house.

Luvella and Uncle Isaac cantered down Mountain Road, toward the Valley. Avoiding the merchants' area, they took the road to Daddy's sawmill, then turned to climb the road following the creeks north toward Forksville.

Uncle Isaac led the way, pushing the horses to a gallop, but as the road became steeper, he slowed a little. "I want to get past Eagles Mere before we stop for lunch. So, if you can do it, we can gallop some, then slow to a canter. The horses should hold up at that pace."

"I'm right with you, Uncle Isaac," Luvella responded, her voice smooth, even with the rise and fall of her body in the saddle.

Daddy had always told her, "You have good control of your legs in the saddle. Yup. Good strong legs."

Uncle Isaac rode ahead of Luvella in silence. When the sun was high, he stopped and swung one leg over the horse's head to slide to the ground. He came back and helped Luvella jump off her horse. "Let the horses rest a few minutes." He walked to a clear spot where they could see the beautiful woods all around them and a river winding below. Luvella followed. "That's Trout River down there. Runs from Hunter's Lake." He stood and looked at the river for several minutes, then gazed at the mountain of trees rising around it.

Luvella wondered if he were thinking of Aunt Hilda, like she was. She couldn't stop thinking of her and how she would take care of this dying woman.

"My people lived and hunted here just twenty years ago," the old man said, "up until the battle at Wounded Knee changed everything." Silent for several long moments, he finally sighed and changed the subject. "Your Bible tells the story of Noah and his ark. Our people also believe in the great flood where all men perished, but we believe the turtle saved us. The turtle, which can live in water and on land, survived the flood and filled the earth with people again. That is why the Turtle Clan is most important in all our tribes."

Luvella didn't know what to say. Her family didn't

talk about beliefs. They just tried to live them. Isaac turned slowly and walked to Daisy's side, holding his folded hands open for Luvella to stand on and mount her horse. "It is time to go."

In quietude, they galloped, cantered, and walked up the road and around Eagles Mere Lake to its northern tip, where Isaac again studied the water. At the turn of the road, they continued straight, following a trail through the woods. "This is shorter and faster," Uncle Isaac explained.

The trail was wide enough for a wagon to fit between the trees on either side but hadn't been cleared of stones and most tree roots like the road had been. Luvella concentrated on the trail for Daisy's safety, watching for stray rocks, branches, and of course, snakes. The trail ran alongside a creek, and Luvella's thoughts ran amok, like the dancing froth of the rushing water. She inhaled the scent of pines, much stronger here than at home, and she felt exhilarated, heady with her own deep love of the mountains and with Uncle Isaac's tales.

They finally stopped at a campsite between the trail and the creek. A huge boulder, almost flat on the top, nestled in the sun at the side of the creek and Luvella headed toward it.

"Luvella." Isaac said in a loud, sharp whisper. She turned to him. He nodded toward the boulder, and she looked at it again. A rattlesnake, more than three feet long and as big around as Daddy's arm, curled around the small crevices of the rock, sunning itself. Its yellowish-brown color blended in with the shades of tan and brown of the boulder, but Luvella could see it distinctly now. She had disturbed it, and it lifted its head, coiled its body into a layered circle with amazing speed, and flicked its tongue out and in, out and in. It lifted its tail and shook it, sounding the tell-tale rattle that gave the snake its name.

Luvella thought of Daddy's parting words, "Don't go into the woods without protection." She backed slowly toward Daisy, not taking her eyes off the snake. She hoped to reach her saddlebag and Daddy's pistol. *Can I outrace the rattler? Or will it spook Daisy away first, taking the gun away from me?*

Uncle Isaac whispered, but his voice was desperate. "Don't move, Luvella. Stand still."

Luvella stopped.

The snake uncurled from its resting nook on the rock and slithered into the brush. Uncle Isaac walked over to her. "You are a brave young maiden."

Luvella stood straight. "Yes, as long as I don't see a snake." They chuckled together.

Uncle Isaac said, "My people believe that what we do to anything on Mother Earth, we do to ourselves, for we are all one." His eyes, peering through the canopy of trees, scanned the sky. "A rattler won't attack you unless it feels cornered. But you should always be alert in the forest for critters. This is their home.

"I think it's cooler and safer to rest right in the campsite area," Uncle Isaac said. "Let's tie the horses firmly in case something else comes along. I will tell you about rattlesnakes while we eat."

Luvella tugged at Daisy's reins, all the while darting looks here and there, and led the horse to a tree with thick, low branches. Isaac walked slowly, leaving his horse tethered at a nearby tree, and inspected the area. He shuffled and scuffed to announce to any nearby animals that people were here.

They sat on a section of large log that lay on the ground in front of a cold fire pit. Luvella had pulled out their lunch and untied the corners of the cloth. Thick slices of Mama's bread were on top. Underneath the bread were slabs of the beef roast left over from last night's dinner. A small jar of Mama's apple butter sat next to the meat on the two pie tins holding the food. Luvella gave one pie tin to Uncle Isaac and kept the other one.

She opened the jar of apple butter and sniffed. Cinnamon, nutmeg, and applesauce filled her nostrils.

Isaac laughed. "Your Aunt Hilda used to make apple butter, too. Nothin' like it, is there?"

Luvella grinned, passing a knife to him. "Mama told me it was her mama's recipe, so this should taste just like Aunt Hilda's."

Isaac tasted the apple butter and smiled. "It is the same recipe." They shared the food and ate hungrily.

"Rattlesnakes are interesting creatures," Isaac began. "My grandfather told me a rattler can stare at an animal's or person's eyes and put them in a trance. Then the rattler can attack with no resistance from the animal." He bit a healthy piece of beef from his slice and followed that with some bread. "I think that's more myth than truth. But a rattlesnake won't waste its precious venom on you unless you're making it feel in danger. Usually, it will crawl away, just like you saw here." He nodded toward the rock.

Luvella smiled weakly. "I'll try to remember all that the next time one scares me to death."

When they finished eating, they walked to the creek and used the pie tins to scoop water for drinking.

Uncle Isaac pointed to some purple-flowered plants growing near the water's edge.

"That's snakeroot," he said. "If you ever get bit by a rattler, I'm sure you already know how to cut a cross through the fang marks and bleed the wound. Then pick one of these flowers and chew its leaves. Swallow the juice and make a poultice with the chewed leaves." He shook his pie tin free of water. "Hold the poultice to the bite with some cloth, and it will draw the poison out. You can chew the roots of the flower, too, and you can also make a tea with the leaves. This plant is good for all kinds of wounds." He nodded at her, smiled, and walked back to the horses.

On the rest of the trip, Luvella noticed Uncle Isaac was pushing the horses—and her—a little harder, faster. He was eager to get home before dark, but she was sure he wanted even more to be with Aunt Hilda. By nightfall, the snakes may be tucked in for the night, but the bobcats and bear would be out looking for food.

Luvella's thoughts wandered, from the Basket Bonanza, to the convention, to Mr. Bocke, and finally back to Aunt Hilda. *What will she be like. How will I know what to do for her?*

Then she remembered the typhoid, how she had taken care of Reeder, who was crazy with the fever, and Mama, who looked like death had already come to take her away. And she was two years younger when her whole family had the typhoid. She could certainly take care of Aunt Hilda. But I've never nursed a dying person before, she argued with herself.

Uncle Isaac slowed a little and stopped at a clearing, interrupting her silent argument. "Let's just walk around a little. The horses are thirsty, too, I reckon."

When Isaac helped her down from Daisy, Luvella could feel her knees wanting to continue to bend, but she stood straight and strong. *Daddy would be proud of me*. "Feels good to walk, Uncle Isaac." She led Daisy down the incline to the creek. The sun was just beginning to dip behind the trees on the other side of the creek. *Our stops for rests and food have taken longer than I thought*. Both she and Uncle Isaac leaned over, scooped water into their hands, and slurped noisily.

Isaac stood then, pointing due north. "There's the road to Forksville just yonder. My house is this side of the town, so we don't have much farther to go. And the ride will be easier now."

Luvella smiled, saying nothing. *That's a relief. A nice hot supper and a clean bed will feel really good. And my knees don't feel as strong as Daddy told me they were.*

The thoughts of food and bed clung to Luvella's mind like moss to a tree. But every time she saw a curl of gray smoke above the timberline, she worried about what lay ahead of her. *What can I possibly do for Aunt Hilda?*

Finally, Uncle Isaac left the road and led her through a very narrow trail into a wide yard. Yellow light glowed through one front window of a log house. The trail led around the house to a barn in back, very similar to Luvella's own barn.

The front door of the house opened briskly, and a young man loped to the horses. "Uncle Isaac! Welcome." He took Kitschi's reins and reached for Daisy's. He wasn't much older than she, perhaps seventeen or eighteen, dark brown hair and eyes, just a hint of Indian blood. And very good looking! She looked away quickly when his eyes looked up to meet hers.

"Luke, this is my niece on Hilda's side, Luvella. She's going to help Hilda. Her mama is sickly and couldn't come." Isaac waved his arm from one to the other. "Luvella, Luke is my sister's grandson, as I already told you. He helps me a lot around here."

Luke let go of Daisy's reins and reached up to help Luvella off her horse. She couldn't avoid letting him lift her down without being very rude; neither could she prevent the rush of blood to her face. Fortunately, she figured he couldn't see the blush in the fading sunlight. But what triggered her most upsetting embarrassment was that her knees buckled when her feet hit the ground. Luke's hands, one under each of her arms, held her up with absolutely no sign of effort. She mustered every ounce of energy to straighten her legs.

Luvella's mind raced. *What is behind those lighted windows for me? And why is this Luke boy here? Oh, Mama! What have you done to me?* She released one loud sob, as if she were in pain.

Luke held her more firmly. "Are you hurt?"

Luvella shook her head, pushed away from him, and swallowed hard. "I'm fine," she said softly, and turned to unbuckle her saddlebag.

Uncle Isaac came over to Daisy. "Luke, would you take care of the horses? Luvella and I could use a good meal!"

## Chapter Eight

The coolness of the long room raised goosebumps on her arms as she entered from the porch, and she realized how warm she had been, riding the trail to Forksville. The smells coming from the kitchen made her stomach growl as Uncle Isaac excused himself to go to Aunt Hilda.

A young woman emerged from the kitchen, wiping her hands on her apron. She smiled as she waddled toward Luvella and reached to carry the saddlebag. Luvella couldn't help but notice the large bulge underneath her apron.

"I'm Luvella, come to help Aunt Hilda," she said simply.

The woman's smile broadened. "I've been waiting dinner on you and Uncle Isaac. I'm Hannah. Welcome!"

"Thank you, Hannah. The dinner smells…mmm…so good. It's making my empty stomach rumble."

Hannah laughed. She was taller than Luvella, but Luvella thought she wasn't much older than she, maybe nineteen or twenty. Her long black hair shone like a pond in moonlight, and her face was slender, smooth, and fine-cut. "Luke caught a 'coon yesterday morning, so it's been on the stove most of today. I cooked it with fresh tomatoes and garlic and onions, so it ought to be good."

"Ooohhh," Luvella said. "I haven't had raccoon in a long time. My brothers have been too busy at the sawmill to hunt much, I guess."

Hannah pointed toward a doorway off the other side of the dining-sitting room they were in. "Let's get you settled." She carried the saddlebag to the bedroom. "I didn't get the pitcher on the commode filled with water yet."

Luvella took back her saddlebag from Hannah. "I'll carry this. And I can wash in the kitchen for now. Don't worry about me.

"How is Aunt Hilda?" Luvella searched Hannah's face, which immediately turned serious.

Hannah shook her head. "She sleeps, a very deep sleep. She never moves or makes a sound, day or night."

Isaac came into the dining room just as Luke entered the house. A look of warmth and respect passed between the man and boy, and Luke was, indeed, almost as tall as Isaac. Although his shoulders were broad, Luke had the lean look of a spring buck.

Uncle Isaac said, "Luvella, let's have dinner before I take you in to Hilda. You deserve a little rest after our long ride."

Luvella nodded, and when Luke glanced her way, she quickly headed toward the kitchen. She washed her face and hands at the sink. "Hannah what can I do to help you?"

Hannah smiled and sighed. "Oh, thank you." She handed the masher over. "You can mash the potatoes. Doing that is a real botheration to my back." She put her right hand on the small of her back and leaned back a little, making the baby-bulge stick out even more. A few moments later, Luvella felt truly welcome, at home, as she carried the platters and bowls of food to the table.

The raccoon was very tender, immersed with garden-fresh carrots in the thick and spicy tomato sauce. Luvella even put some of the sauce on her mashed potatoes. The dinner and biscuits, hot from the oven, brought happiness once more to her stomach.

Isaac chatted during dinner, telling Hannah and Luke about Luvella's family. "Will and Margaret made me feel just like family. And Luvella here, she's a bobcat in business. Wait till I tell you about her plans for Muncy Valley." He raised his eyebrows and nodded. "She is the village princess."

Luvella blushed, feeling chastised. *Does he think I'm pampered?*

Luke spoke up. "You understand that's a compliment, don't you? A princess of an Indian village is very responsible and highly respected."

She looked at him and realized she should respond. "Uhhh, yes. Thank you, Uncle Isaac." *Why can't I think right when that boy looks at me?*

When Luvella noticed that there would be no dessert—Mama almost always had something for dessert—she took another biscuit and buttered it generously. Then, as she and Hannah carried some of the dinner dishes to the kitchen, Luvella whispered to Hannah, "Would you come with me to see Aunt Hilda?"

"Sure," Hannah said softly. "Let's do it now. We can wash the dishes afterward. Uncle Isaac, shall we take Luvella in to meet Aunt Hilda now?"

Uncle Isaac had settled into a large overstuffed chair in the sitting area. He looked up and studied Luvella. "I think it is time." He stood and led the way to his wife's bedroom.

Luvella's dinner rolled inside her. She swallowed a huge lump that suddenly lodged in her throat, and her heart pounded at her chest. Hannah's hand, placed lightly on the back of her shoulder, brought her courage, and she smiled a thanks to her new friend.

The bedroom was softly lit by one window, which let the orange afterglow of the sunset cast a golden radiance on everything, even the wasted figure in the bed. A small, gray face, whose skin hung loosely over cheeks and jaw, lay death-like on an embroidered pillowcase. White-gold hair cascaded around it. A quilt, sewn in the wedding ring pattern with fabric in different shades of blue, pink, and tiny flowers, covered the barely discernable form.

Luvella walked to the side of the bed, near her aunt's head. She swallowed again. *I will be strong.*

"Hello, Aunt Hilda. I'm Luvella, Margaret's youngest daughter." *Did I see something move under the covers? No, I'm just spooked.* "I'm here to take care of you in Mama's place. She's been sick with pneumonia and could not come." *She is moving! Her hand, I think.*

"Mama sends her love, and I am very happy to help you, Aunt Hilda." Luvella rested her hands on the bed, peered at the quilt, and then at her face.

Aunt Hilda turned her head and shoulders toward Luvella, pulled her arms out from under the quilt, and reached out to her. Luvella stood like stone, but her head moved to glance quickly at Hannah.

Hannah's brows furrowed, and she looked ready to cry.

One of Aunt Hilda's hands was holding something, which she pressed into Luvella's hand and covered it with her own. She spoke unintelligible words, babbling actually. "Duh, buh duh buh…" But the tone of those sounds, the way she moved her head, and the intensity of her expression told Luvella of her great-aunt's love and gratitude.

Uncle Isaac and Hannah, who had been standing at the foot of the bed, rushed to Luvella's side as Aunt Hilda sank back to her pillow.

"Hilda!" Uncle Isaac said, his voice desperate.

Hannah looked at Luvella, her mouth agape, and whispered, "She hasn't made a single sound or moved even one finger in at least a week."

Aunt Hilda remained motionless, eyes closed, face in silent repose. The quilt rose and fell, just barely, with the old woman's slow, shallow breaths. Uncle Isaac took her hands and gently placed them under the covers again. He looked down at Luvella. "She has spoken to you from the Spirit World. You have pleased her, Luvella, and the Great Spirit as well, I think. I will sit with her for a while now."

Luvella looked at her hand, still gripping what Aunt Hilda had given her. Isaac and Hannah focused there also. As she opened her fingers, a little clothespin doll rolled to its side. Ugly. Obviously hand made by a child.

"That's what she's had in her hand all week. I couldn't pry it open," Hannah said. "She must have been waiting to give it to you."

Isaac said, "That's the doll she's saved all these

years, the one your mama made for her, Luvella, when your mama was only about five or six. Hilda loved that little doll."

Both Hannah and Luvella were quiet throughout redding the table and rinsing the dishes. It was a hallowed, hushed quiet, like in the mountain just before a rainstorm. Unwilling to break the spell, Luvella barely whispered, "I will wash and dry the dishes. You go home while there is still a little light."

"Yes, I'll go home." She hugged Luvella. "I will stop for a visit with you tomorrow. I want to know this special niece of Aunt Hilda's better." She smiled.

Hannah set off on foot. With dusk approaching, Luke accompanied her home, saying he'd return later. Uncle Isaac's soft chanting floated into the kitchen from Aunt Hilda's bedside. "Hiy-yuh, huh-yuh…" The rest of the song faded into whispers.

Luvella washed and dried the dishes. Afterward, she ran out to the privy before the blackness of night descended, then went into her assigned bedroom and took a change of clothes from the saddlebag. She shook out the wrinkles and hung the dress and shawl on the hooks in the clothes press, noting the river, wheat, and sun carvings on its door. She placed her clean chemise, drawers, and stockings in the drawer of the commode and laid her nightgown on the bed. Then she took the pitcher to the kitchen, primed the pump, and filled the pitcher with water. She couldn't help but grunt a little as she carried the filled pitcher back to the bedroom and placed it in the bowl on top of the commode. She was glad Luke wasn't there to hear her grunt. She noticed a clean towel on the side rack of the commode and thought how nice Hannah had been to her this evening.

When she heard Uncle Isaac's continued soft chants—*or were they Indian prayers?*—she wandered through the dining room and out onto the porch. The crickets were singing their pulsating harmonies, the bullfrogs were croaking from a pond or creek that must be nearby, and one lonely cicada was still buzzing its way out of its shell. *How strange. The world is so alive out here and in the house...hmmm, what is in the house?*

*I don't want to say death is there because Hannah, the new baby inside her, and Uncle Isaac are very alive. Even Aunt Hilda proved she's still alive. But I feel a different kind of life when I'm in there, like when I talk to my mountain.*

An image came to mind of her standing on the side of the mountain amidst trees fifty feet tall, their tops, silhouetted against a brilliant blue sky, rustling softly in a gentle breeze. She feels their life, their energy when she's there. And their response when she talks to them. She shook her head. *Maybe I'm feeling the presence of the baby, Hannah's baby.*

"You are a happy mystery to my family." The voice startled Luvella, and she jumped. From the side of the house, Luke leapt over the railing and onto the porch, barely making a thud. "Sorry I scared you."

"You didn't scare me," Luvella retorted.

He stood next to her, and in the glow from the dining room lantern light, Luvella could see the puzzled look on his face.

"I'm sorry," he repeated.

"That's all right." Luvella couldn't think of one other sensible thing to say, so she turned and opened the screen door into the house.

"Good night," he called to her back.

She continued walking, straight and stiff, across the dining room into her bedroom. She scooped up the quilt covering the bed, her nightgown with it, and walked to Aunt Hilda's room. Uncle Isaac was quiet, so Luvella entered the room.

"I can stay with her now, Uncle Isaac. You should get some rest."

Uncle Isaac stood and looked at her and then the quilt.

"I'll sleep right here in the chair," she said. "Aunt Hilda will not be alone."

Isaac smiled, then reached down to touch Hilda's head and to slide his hand down her cheek, holding his hand there for a moment. He left the room in silence.

Luvella walked to Aunt Hilda's bedside, where she had stood just a little while before. "This is Luvella again, Aunt Hilda," she said softly. "Mama told me to tell you she has missed you all these years, and she loves you very much. I wish so much that I'd gotten to know you." She studied Aunt Hilda's face for any sign of awareness, of having heard her words. But there was no movement, no frown or raised eyebrows, just the slow, slight rise and fall of her breathing.

"It's funny," Luvella murmured. "Last night at supper, Mama was telling us about that clothespin doll she'd made for you. She laughed and told us it was the ugliest doll she'd ever seen, but you just loved it and treasured it." Luvella swallowed noisily and brushed her eyes. "Aunt Hilda, this will be the most loved ugly doll in the whole world." She started to chuckle, but it turned into a sob. "It will be held in your honor for all of Mama's and my whole life." She backed down to the foot of Hilda's bed.

"I'll be sleeping right here at the foot of your bed, Aunt Hilda. Mama's heart is with us, I know, so the three of us are all together. And if what Uncle Isaac said is true, maybe the Great Spirit is with us, too."

Luvella changed into her nightgown, pulled the chair close so she could rest her feet on the bed to feel any movement of Aunt Hilda's during the night. She snuggled into the chair under the quilt and, with a sliver of light shining through the slight opening of the door, examined the doll in her hand.

The wooden clothespin had two painted dots on the front of its top for eyes, an upturned arc just below the eyes for its mouth, and a faded piece of red and white gingham tied to its middle to give the dress effect. Luvella smiled. Clutching the doll to her chest, she closed her eyes and tried not to think of the events of the day. Especially the Luke events.

## Chapter Nine

The murmured sounds of Uncle Isaac's deep tones and Luke's husky voice wafted into Aunt Hilda's bedroom like a muted lullaby. Their voices blended with Aunt Hilda's shallow breaths, creating a hazy background for Luvella. She burrowed into the chair and a deep, exhausted sleep.

Hours later, as early morning light pried open Luvella's eyelids, it took her only seconds to remember she was in Aunt Hilda's room. Her muscles, stiff from yesterday's long ride and from sitting in the chair all night, began to cramp when she tried to stretch them. Her legs and back were tight, but she didn't want to move them and disturb Aunt Hilda. She sat up slowly and frowned. *Something* was very different.

Aunt Hilda was there, still not moving. But… But…*she wasn't breathing!*

The absence of sound in the room wrapped Luvella like a shroud. Wide awake now, she pulled her legs from the bed and stood. She put her hand, the one not holding the doll, on Aunt Hilda's blanketed arm and then up to rest on her aunt's forehead.

"Oh, Aunt Hilda." She gulped the sob that was choking her. "I should have been here earlier for you. What have our families missed all these years?" She rubbed Hilda's forehead and pushed the hair back from her face—a face that looked remarkably like Mama's across the forehead and eyes.

Tears streamed down Luvella's cheeks as she continued to rub her aunt's forehead. "Aunt Hilda, I wish so much I had known you. Now the only thing left to say is goodbye." She pulled her hand back and wiped the tears from her face. "Mama says goodbye to you, too." Luvella picked up the doll she had dropped on the bed. "Aunt Hilda, Mama and I will both treasure this doll for our whole lives, so in a way, we'll always be together."

She stood by the bed, not knowing what to do next. A knot had formed in her stomach, and she felt a powerful urge to sob. *Oh, I mustn't cry in front of all these people, especially poor Uncle Isaac.* She suddenly realized that Aunt Hilda's head had felt warm. *She must have just now died. That's what woke me up—her* not *breathing!*

Luvella searched the room and saw her clothes folded on top of the commode. She rushed over and grabbed them, clutching them inside the blanket she wrapped around herself. *Uncle Isaac. I have to get Uncle Isaac.*

Once in the dining room, her eyes lifted up to the loft. "Uncle Isaac," she said, her voice wobbly with suppressed tears. A low rumble of deep breathing answered her. "Uncle Isaac!" she repeated, loudly this time, her voice gaining strength.

There was silence again as the breathing sounds stopped; Luvella waited. Then Uncle Isaac leaped from his bed to the railing. "Is it Hilda?" He disappeared to the back of the loft, not needing an answer. When he raced down the stairs, his shirt was billowing behind him, his suspenders hanging loosely at his sides. He took long strides directly into Aunt Hilda's room.

Luvella followed him and waited at the door, watching because she didn't know what else to do. Uncle Isaac stood at Aunt Hilda's side for a brief second. He threw himself across the bed, his face buried in Hilda's blanket, his shoulders heaving. Luvella remembered Mama's shoulders shaking with sobs, too, that awful day when Bessie's baby had lost his battle with the typhoid. *Was that two years ago already?*

Luvella had had the same sense of exclusion then, too. Each family member had experienced his or her own raw grief as she was left to grieve alone, in her own solitary way.

She left her uncle so he could mourn in private. She went to her room, washed up, and dressed as quickly as she could. *I'll do what I did then—I'll keep busy. Things need to be done; I'll do them. The emptiness in my heart will just have to wait.* She fought back tears and hurried to the kitchen. *Feeling sorry for yourself won't help.* She began preparing breakfast, stoking the stove fire for coffee first. She found the battered tin coffee pot, pumped water into it, and looked around the unfamiliar kitchen. *What to make for breakfast?*

She found the coffee and then the flour. *Flapjacks.* She grabbed a basket from a stack near the door and went out to gather eggs from the hen house and milk and bacon from the springhouse.

She raced back to the house, hesitating, listening, once she was inside the door. Uncle Isaac was whispering and humming his sad songs in Aunt Hilda's room. Luvella rushed into the kitchen and scurried from cupboard to table to stove.

*Why do I feel so…so abandoned?* The coffee was perking, and it seemed like only seconds had passed before the bacon was sizzling. *I hardly knew Aunt Hilda. But I feel like I've lost a part of me…a part of my soul.*

She poured some of the bacon grease onto the hot griddle and arranged three equal dollops of flapjack batter on it.

She thought of the wedding ring pattern, the intertwining circles, on Aunt Hilda's quilt. *We are connected.* She nodded as she watched the circles of flapjacks spread into each other. *We are connected by blood, but Aunt Hilda's coming out of her deep sleep to hold my hands…that's a connection of love. How I wish I'd known her.*

Luvella raised her shoulders in a huge sigh and looked about her. She had never in her life prepared any meal so quickly. She felt like a log on a mountain stream, current-driven to the waterfall. The closer she came to the deadly precipice, the faster the tide carried her. She knew the day ahead of her would be awful, and she couldn't keep it from happening, no matter how fast she worked.

"I *thought* I smelled bacon," Luke said.

Luvella jumped. She had been so immersed in her thoughts that she hadn't heard the door open.

"Oh! I'm sorry," Luke said. "I seem to have a talent for startling you." He didn't give her a chance to reply. His smile faded when he saw her face, and his became serious, a concerned frown pinching his brows together. He looked toward Aunt Hilda's room and Uncle Isaac's chants. "Did Aunt Hilda…"

Luvella nodded. Neither she nor Luke said the word die.

Luke hesitated for only a second, then moved quickly to his uncle. Luvella knew he would bring comfort to the old man. She stood by the sink, looking out the window at the rows of corn and tomato plants growing in the large garden behind the house, and hugged herself. *What am I supposed to do today?*

Luke returned, shuffling his feet, deliberately, Luvella was sure, so she had no trouble hearing his approach. "I'll go get Hannah to help you." His face was flushed, and in his eyes Luvella thought she saw moisture. *Had he been crying?*

Luvella turned. "Oh, that would be so nice," she said. "I'd be really grateful. But let me fix you a plate of breakfast first."

They ate together in silence, although each was so engrossed in thought and sorrow, neither noticed. Finally, Luvella spoke. "I will not let Hannah do any work today. I know, in her condition, she shouldn't be taking care of Aunt Hilda. But she can tell me what I should do."

Luke nodded and rose. "I'll bring her back very soon. She doesn't live far from here. Other women from our tribe will come later."

When he left, Luvella began clearing the table. She picked the remaining eggs from the basket and put them into another basket suspended from the ceiling near the window.

As she picked up the basket she had used to gather eggs to put it back by the door, she felt the heft of it, its sturdiness. The straw was tightly woven, which gave the basket its strength, and there were colored designs entwined along the sides. *This is one of the baskets Uncle Isaac was telling us about!* She strode across the dining room to the door and examined the others. They were beautiful. Each one was a little different. There were different sizes, different designs, different colors.

She was still looking at them when Uncle Isaac walked into the room. His shirt was buttoned now and tucked into his trousers, the suspenders doing their job over his shoulders. His feet were still bare. He walked noiselessly to the coffeepot and filled a mug he had picked up from the table.

Luvella rushed to his side, resting her hand on his arm. "Uncle Isaac, I am so sorry." She brought her arm back, embarrassed she had touched him. "Sit down, Uncle Isaac. You'll need a good breakfast to carry you through."

She hurried into the kitchen and noticed he was following her command; he sat at the table. *Oh, Hannah. Please hurry.*

"Luke has gone to get Hannah. She can tell me what to do. I'm sure there are certain preparations to be done now."

Uncle Isaac nodded and sipped his coffee. Luvella started making bread in the kitchen. *We always need bread. And it feels good to work with my hands.* Uncle Isaac ate, alone and quiet. Then he put on his boots and went outside.

Luvella had the bread rising in pans covered with damp cloths and was just drying the dishes when Hannah came in with two women. "This is my mother, Luvella. Mrs. Raven." She gestured toward the woman directly behind her, medium tall, with brown hair pulled to a knot at the nape of her neck. Smile lines around her hazel eyes and mouth spoke of youthful energy more than middle-aged merriment. Her nose was fine-cut and tilted up a little at its end. Luvella couldn't help but notice that Mrs. Raven was not an Indian.

"And this," Hannah continued, pointing to the second woman, "is Mrs. Greycloud, a good friend of Aunt Hilda. They're going to take care of Aunt Hilda and prepare her for her funeral tomorrow."

Mrs. Greycloud was short, almost as short as Luvella, and stout. She had high cheekbones and large, almond-shaped eyes set in smooth, copper skin. The two women went directly to Aunt Hilda's room and began a series of chants. Luvella heard the first few words, which sounded like "Naro-nana Ro-a-nay-a…," but Hannah had work for her to do. She held up a white shirt-like dress, her face serious, unsmiling.

"This is what our people wear to the Spirit World. We need to iron this," Hannah said as she duck-walked, holding her back, to the shed off the kitchen to get the flatirons. "You'd better stoke the fire to get it hot." Together, they placed the flatirons on the stovetop to heat them. Hannah showed Luvella where the ironing board was.

Holding up the long shirt, Hannah explained, "My mother made this for Aunt Hilda to wear now. Mother and Mrs. Greycloud will bathe and dress her and fix her hair." Luvella wet her fingertip and, holding up one flatiron, quickly and lightly tapped her wet fingertip on it. The hiss told her the iron was hot enough, and she began to iron.

As she ironed, Hannah told her what to expect. "Some women will come tonight to mourn Aunt Hilda. It is our Muncee tradition." Luvella saw a hint of pride in Hannah's face. "But, of course, we cannot let Forksville people know that we are practicing our customs.

"And some other Muncee women, maybe the same ones, too, will come at dawn tomorrow to mourn," Hannah continued. "The minister from the Methodist church will come to lead his service, and there will be a short Muncee ceremony at the gravesite later in the morning. The men will bury her after that. They're probably building the coffin right now." She exhaled a long sigh.

"Hannah," Luvella said. "I think you were probably very close to Aunt Hilda. I'm sorry for you. I know you'll miss her."

Hannah nodded, bowing her head and clenching her lips together. She ambled over to the stove and uncovered the bread, which had risen to mounds over the edges of the bread pans.

*They look like tiny graves!* Luvella thought.

Hannah floured her hand and punched each mound of dough, then pulled in the surrounding dough to make each a level loaf again, and turned them over, ready for the second rising. She pumped a little water onto the cloths, wrung them well, and replaced them on the bread loaves.

After the older women had dressed Aunt Hilda in her freshly ironed shirt and prepared her for her new life, they joined Hannah and Luvella in the kitchen for some coffee. Uncle Isaac and Luke came in, and the older adults made plans for both the funerals. The required Christian funeral service would be first, to satisfy the local government. And after the minister left, they would secretly hold the Muncee ceremony, just as

Hannah had told Luvella. After the decisions, a quiet descended on them as they each examined their coffee mugs in earnest.

Luvella dared to take their minds off Aunt Hilda for a few moments. "Uncle Isaac, I think I collected all the eggs this morning. I'll check again to make sure. I used one of those baskets by the door. Was that all right?"

Isaac turned to look at them. "Oh yes, Luvella. We use them for everything we need to collect outdoors." He spoke of *we*, of Hilda and him, as if it would always be *we*. People all around the table stared at their mugs again.

"The basket is the strongest and most beautiful I've ever seen," Luvella continued, and waited. She didn't want to be too bold, or to appear to not respect their grief. But it worked. Uncle Isaac looked up at her, his eyes suddenly glimmering with a thought, an idea completely separate from his wife, or his loss of her.

"Elizabeth here made the two top ones." He gestured at Mrs. Raven, Hannah and Luke's mother. "Martha made others"—he nodded toward the other woman—"and Hilda made the ones by the window. All those baskets are the kinds I was telling you about for your festival."

Luvella smiled. "Oh, I was hoping that."

Quiet returned to the table, and Luvella went outside to check for more eggs. It felt good to get out in the sunshine.

The women stayed for dinner and afterward went immediately into Hilda's room. As they sang, "Coll ah ja na jah da nah jo..." Luvella heard weeping and someone was sobbing. This lasted for several hours.

Hannah explained softly to Luvella as they worked in the kitchen. "My people believe that it is necessary for us to mourn. It helps rid our bodies of our grief, and it frees Aunt Hilda's spirit to move on to the Spirit World." She explained that the women would come back at dawn to mourn some more, and the funeral would probably take place about ten o'clock in the morning.

"The funeral—our funeral—will be short but beautiful, Luvella," she continued. "Aunt Hilda will be placed in a coffin and covered with a cloth. The men will place the coffin so Aunt Hilda's head faces east and her feet point to the west. The sun rises in the east and brings us knowledge and spirituality. The west brings us the Spirit World and the rains that sustain our crops. The prayers will fill in the details for you tomorrow." She dried her hands on the towel. "And later, after eating much food, we will dance. Our people dance for every occasion, every chance we get." She smiled as her eyes brimmed.

"Right now, I think we both ought to get to bed. Dawn comes very early!"

Luvella went outside with Hannah and stood watching her leave. She walked with a straight back, like Luke, even with the heaviness in her belly. Luvella's gaze wandered over the yard. *I wonder where Luke is?* She hadn't seen him since this morning. *I'm sure he'll be here tomorrow. I will have to talk to him, to tell him I'm sorry for his loss. I think losing Aunt Hilda is very hard for him.*

She couldn't get to sleep right away, especially with the chanting coming from Aunt Hilda's room. "Pay ya ah ha ya… Oy ya ca la..." But after a while, it was the chanting that lulled her to sleep.

The next morning, after the minister's prayers and blessing, the men carried the coffin on their shoulders, Luke among them. Luvella noticed his shoulders, broad and straight. His eyes caught and held hers for a moment, and completely unaware, she thought of what it must have been like for Aunt Hilda to fall in love with Uncle Isaac. *She had to give up her family and her whole life as it had been.*

As the crowd gathered around the burial site, the pastor finished his service by reading the Twenty-third Psalm. "The Lord is my Shepherd; I shall not want…" When he finished, he blessed the grave and left. When he was gone and confirmed to be out of earshot, someone played a plaintive melody on a flute while a young man beat a steady, slow rhythm on a drum.

Luvella closed her eyes. The music, the soft pulse of the drum, the warmth of the sun, and the gentle kiss of the breeze lifted her heart, her spirits. At that moment, she was sure Aunt Hilda was safe at home with the Great Spirit, the same Great Spirit Luvella prayed to every Sunday with Mama and Daddy.

A gray-haired man, whom everyone treated with much respect, spoke about the powers of the north, south, east, and west, and also of earth and sky. *I speak to my mountain every day. Am I feeling those powers? Deep down, do I believe as these people do?*

After the men lowered the coffin into the deep hole and filled it with dirt, Uncle Isaac lifted his head toward the sun and said in his deepest orotund voice, "Oh Great Spirit, I thank you for the six powers of the universe." Then he turned and led everyone back to his house.

## Chapter Ten

The sun was still low in the east when Luvella hugged Uncle Isaac goodbye and mounted Daisy for her trip back home. She had said her farewell to Hannah last evening, and an awkward goodbye to Luke. Uncle Isaac detailed for her instructions on the best and shortest route to her home, and Luvella concentrated on those as she pressed Daisy to a canter. Once she reached the creek-side trail, she knew the rest of the way would be easy.

She insisted, against Uncle Isaac's offers of help, on going back alone. Leaving so early in the morning assured her of an early afternoon arrival home. Now, as the woods closed around her and the narrow trail, she questioned her wisdom. She reached down and patted her saddlebag, feeling Daddy's pistol and the voluminous lunch Uncle Isaac had urged her to pack, and was reassured. Nonetheless, she looked about her with a sharp eye and smoothed Daisy's mane to give the horse some of the confidence that she, herself, did not feel.

The trail was level for the first hour, and Luvella began thinking about the previous day. She had to admit she enjoyed the after-funeral activities, although she felt some guilt about that now. Hannah stayed close to her, and Luke was never very far away. The people there alternately laughed and cried as they talked about their special times with Hilda.

Earlier yesterday afternoon, Luvella had felt Luke's gaze follow her when she helped set the table with the food the women had brought or when she pretended to be examining baskets. She smiled now, reliving the sense of power that had given her. She walked from kitchen to table, to the sink, to the stove, and whenever she checked, she found him watching her. *But maybe that's not because he's taken with me.* The smile disappeared. *Maybe he's just trying to figure out why I'm so mean to him.*

*Oh glory!* She hadn't expected that confession. *I don't* mean *to be mean... I just can't think right when he's around me.* She shook her head, as if to brush away a fly.

In the evening, everyone danced a slow, somber dance around a bonfire to flute and drum music. *What was it Uncle Isaac had told her? Oh yes, the drums are the heartbeat of Mother Earth. I love how his people are so intertwined with all of nature.*

That slow dance around the fire seemed to be a final goodbye to Aunt Hilda. Hannah pulled Luvella into the circle and motioned Luke to take her other hand, so that they both led her through the steps. Simple steps, moving to the right twice, one step at a time, then right, left, right, left in place. She concentrated on the steps and keeping the rhythm until the sound of the drum and the sound of all the feet stepping on the dry ground were one.

That sound reverberated up through her whole body, filling her with comfort, with peace, and with a kind of joy.

When the drummer increased the beat of the drum,

the flute picked up the pace. The dancers formed two lines, like in a reel. In fact, the whole dance was very much like the reels Luvella had danced at home. Every time Luke's hand had pulled her toward him and then past him in the circle, a queasiness had attacked her stomach. *It sounds like I'm the one who's taken. And I have a business and a festival to run. I do not have time for…for a dalliance.*

That reminded Luvella that she needed to be home to continue planning the festival and she also had to write to Pittsburgh's Chamber of Commerce for more information on the conference. She *chsk-chsked* Daisy to a faster pace. *And let's not forget Mr. Bocke! I keep thinking the railroad won't pay any attention to him. But am I wrong to…to dismiss him? Anna said he seemed so determined. I'd better find out about him when I see Mr. Johannson again—when I check on our festival.*

Mrs. Raven had said to her yesterday, "Luvella, Isaac asked us to get busy with many, many baskets. He said your customers will pay us for the baskets, and that makes us all happy." She smiled, her eyes a light lavender with intensity.

A group of women surrounded Mrs. Raven and her. "Do you want certain colors?" "What size do you think is best?" "Do you want flat or round bottoms?" Luvella sensed their eagerness, and probably their need, for added income.

She laughed at their enthusiasm. "I think *you* are the basket experts, so *you* decide the kinds you want to make. I'll try to have the business people in Muncy Valley sell as many as possible. But I think these baskets will be very popular and will sell themselves."

Her mind vaulted back to the conference. *I wonder if I should mention our bonanza in my letter to the Pittsburgh Chamber? Would it make them more open to our participation in the conference? Oops! I told Mama I'd just go and listen, didn't I?*

*Oh, Luvella. The bonanza, the conference, your caboose...what else will you start?* She felt her face wreathed in a big smile now as Daisy cantered along. The sun sneaked through leafy openings in the trees, and she remembered again the prayers and the respect her Indian relative—Uncle Isaac—and his friends had for the earth and the sky. The warmth of the sun penetrated her, blending with the heat of the ride, the leather-squeak of the saddle, and she felt a bit sleepy.

Suddenly, Daisy's shoulders and flank tensed. A whinny of danger came too late to alert Luvella; Daisy reared. Luvella clamped her knees to the horse's flanks. She lunged forward, clutching her arms around Daisy's neck. But Daisy stood tall as a sapling and pawed the air in front of her, as if climbing a wall to safety. Luvella, fear crawling over her body, sensed Daisy's imbalance. The horse twisted slightly. Luvella felt her own hands and knees unwillingly release. She flailed the mountain air as she was hurtled toward the ground. It was as if she had come to a cliff and was falling to her death over the precipice. A glare of sun blinded her. She heard the rattle.

A scream sent birds flying from the treetops—her scream. One foot hit the ground first with a thud that sent shards of pain through her whole body. Then she landed on her side, her head continuing the spiral until it, too, slammed into the dirt. At the same time, a piercing burn stabbed her on the low side of her other leg. Just as she sensed her consciousness slipping away, Luvella felt the scales of a huge snake slither over her legs. Through the haze of pain and sinking into oblivion, she saw it crawl away.

****

The buzz of a locust and a glint of sun in one eye roused Luvella. She opened both eyes, squinting against the sun, and realized she was lying on the ground. She was on her back, her riding skirt flipped up to her knees. Her legs were at odd angles, and she began to straighten them. Pain shot up both legs, and she sucked in air noisily. Holding herself perfectly still, she grunted her breaths.

*Snake bite!* She remembered the hot stab into her leg. *Oh! I've got to take care of it—fast!* She sat up and groaned, holding the side of her head. She could feel a lump growing there. *How long have I been lying here, I wonder?* She looked up, still holding her head, which was beginning to throb. The sun was well east of high noon. *Good! Not very long at all.*

She looked at her legs. Her left ankle was pushing outward at the buttons of her shoe, so she unbuttoned the shoe and took it off. "Ohhh, unh! Unh!" she cried, clenching her teeth, wreathing her face in a grimace of pain. Immediately, the freed ankle began to swell to an angry-looking puffiness. Luvella touched it all around gently with a fingertip. When she touched the top of her foot, near the left anklebone, she hissed inward and groaned again.

"Well, Luvella," she said for the forest to hear. "You've broken a bone there near your ankle. We'll have to splint it." Then she looked at her other leg. Just above the top of her high-button shoe, inside of the shinbone, were two fang punctures.

"You stinker!" she yelled, wishing the snake would hear her and tremble. And she was glad Mama couldn't hear her. Stinker was not a lady-like word. She looked around for Daisy. "Daisy!" she called. Everything she needed was with Daisy: a knife, the gun, her food, matches for a fire. She had to take care of that snakebite immediately.

"Daisy!" she called again. She heard the familiar snort, telling her Daisy was grazing nearby. "Come on, Daisy," she purred, pursing her lips to make the *tsch* that Daisy loved. Her head pounded, her left ankle throbbed and was almost twice its normal size, and she knew she had to bleed the snakebite *now* or the venom would go through her whole body.

"Daisy! Come on, Girl. I need you!" She clapped her hands together softly, and *tsched* as Daisy ambled closer and closer. "All right, Daisy, steady, Girl," Luvella said to the horse, by her side now. She pulled on the stirrup to help her stand on her bitten leg and patted Daisy's mane to keep the horse calm. She pulled off the saddlebags, holding them across her left arm as she probed them for the knife. She tied Daisy to the tree next to her, set down the saddlebags, and sat on the ground.

"Now comes the hard part, Luvella. You've got to cut that snakebite and suck the blood out." She slid the knife out of its sheath and poised it above the fang marks. She started to press the knife into her skin and groaned. "How can I do this? I can't cut my own leg!" She looked around the forest, half expecting someone to be there and come to help her. She looked back at her leg and noticed a tiny streak of color beginning to trail from one fang mark.

"Oh, no!" The venom was starting to spread already.

She clenched her teeth, grunted loudly to cover her fear, and pushed the tip of the knife into her leg, drawing it across the fang punctures. Blood oozed out. She pulled the tip of the knife up and made a similar cut crosswise to the first one. She dropped the knife on one saddlebag and let her head drop, sobbing for just a few seconds.

"Luvella, stop! You have to be strong," she said, sniveling, but trying desperately to be firm. She bent forward, grateful for once that she had short legs, wiped away the blood with her hand, and started sucking at the wound. The warm blood that rushed into her mouth made her feel sick, and she spit it out fast, gagging. She repeated the steps, sucking, spitting, gagging, until no more blood came forth. She leaned back against the tree, breathing deeply and trying to quiet her stomach.

Pain nagged her, from each leg and from her head. The arm she had fallen on hurt, too, but she thought it was all right. Nothing broken.

"Oh, why didn't I let Uncle Isaac ride back with me?" she said aloud, realizing she was talking a lot to herself in these woods. *Uncle Isaac! That's right. He told me what to do for snakebite on our trip to his house.*

She put the knife between her teeth and turned onto her knees, crawling. "Come on, Daisy. Come with me." She reached up to untie Daisy from the tree. "I'm going to go down to the creek. That's where that snakeroot was growing before. Let's hope it grows all along the creek side."

Even crawling on her hands and knees sent stabs of pain through her left foot if she jarred it at all. *I'll splint it after I wrap my bite.* She squinted her eyes to focus; the sun was glaring off every leaf, every stone, off the water of the creek just ahead, piercing her very brain.

"Luvella, keep moving ahead. You cannot rest until you take care of your wounds." She had to fight the growing desire to close her eyes and let the sleep of pain and snake venom take over.

Straggling clusters of pale purple flowers, which Uncle Isaac had called snakeroot, came into view, and Luvella crawled with renewed resolve. She found a clump of them right next to the stream and sat on a mound of dirt. As she bent her right knee so she could reach the snakebite, her left foot lay outstretched, and she rested it in the cold creek. The instant relief told her that cold water would be one of her ankle treatments.

She chewed the leaves of some snakeroot. "Swallow some of the snakeroot juice, Luvella," Uncle Isaac had advised. "It wards off the stomach sickness." Grimacing, Luvella took one swallow of the juice and spit out the rest of the mixture into her hand. She wadded the paste into a poultice and placed it on her leg over the bite. "How am I going to keep it there now?" she asked herself, and looked around her. Finally, she had to settle on using her knife to tear off a strip from the bottom of her shirtwaist. She would need more strips for her ankle.

A pine bough, thick with offshoots, was lying on the ground near her, and she used it as a tray to hold many more snakeroot leaves that she could prepare into poultice later. *Uncle Isaac said to use the root of the flower, too.* She dug with her knife around three of the flowers and pulled up the roots, swished the dirt off them in the creek water, and laid them on the pine bough with the leaves. *I think I should dry out some of the leaves for tea—he said that would help me fight the nausea.*

She sat still a moment, resisting the urge to sleep, and looked around her. *I need some sticks for a splint, something to hold my foot straight.* Branches of varying sizes and pieces of wood lay helter-skelter on the forest floor. *And firewood. I'd better get everything together now. I think I'll feel pretty awful as the day wears on.*

Although it seemed like hours had passed, Luvella saw that it wasn't quite noon; the sun was not yet at its high spot. She gathered tinder and some larger pieces of wood, enough for a fire for the whole night. She was leaning on her saddle against a tree, a pile of soft pine boughs underneath it and her. She had scattered leaves over the boughs for added softness. The creek was just a few feet away so she could cool her ankle in it often and wash the sweat from her face. She had filled her tin cup with water to make some snakeroot tea later. Daisy was tied securely just steps away from her, and she had the gun resting in her lap.

*Now I can sleep for a little while.* She rested her ankle up on a log, which relieved the throbbing somewhat. Her other leg, with the snakebite, was aching and turning red. *I think I got most of the venom out, thank goodness.* The poultice seemed to have taken the sharp stinging pain away. But now, Luvella could feel her heart racing, a typical snakebite reaction, and she knew a very bumpy trail lay ahead of her. Although she believed the snakeroot would help ward off the severe reactions to snakebite and possible death, she would still suffer fever and nausea and maybe even the tremors.

The sun was setting when Luvella stirred, pain knifing her to wakefulness. She sat upright slowly, the forest spinning around her. Her stomach reminded her that she hadn't eaten since breakfast, but nausea curled around it. *I have to think. I* must *take care of myself. And Daisy.*

She selected a match from her pile of supplies at her side and lit the tinder. A campfire began to grow, timidly at first. Luvella untied and brought Daisy with her as she crawled to the creek. Both drank the water; Luvella splashed some on her face to cool herself. Her skin felt very hot to the touch. She had pulled her other pair of drawers from her saddlebag and let them soak in the creek. Then she wrung them and, when she was back at her little campsite again, wrapped the cool material around her swollen ankle.

While her tin cup of water was heating on the fire, she chewed some of the snakeroot roots, swallowed a few drops of the juice, scrunching up her face against the bitterness, and placed a fresh poultice on the bitten leg. Then she made a cup of tea with the partially dried leaves, and drank it as she nibbled on a piece of Hannah's bread. The poultice seemed to draw the worst of the pain from the snakebite, and her stomach settled a little after having the tea and bread. She stoked the fire, put one log on it, and settled back, exhausted, against the saddle and tree again.

When she awoke, the woods were black. A soft glow from the fire outlined her ankle, still elevated on the log. An owl hooted nearby. "Whoo-oo. Whoo-oo." Luvella put her hand on the gun and looked all around her. The crickets were singing at a crescendo, so she couldn't hear a bear if there were one. The fire snapped, and she thought her heart would stop.

She rolled some more of the wood she had gathered earlier onto the fire. Flames flared with new exuberance. Even with the fever raging inside her, she welcomed the warmth of the fire and pulled the saddle blanket over her. She started to shiver and heard herself talking nonsense. *Maybe Daddy or Uncle Isaac is coming to rescue me. That's who I hear talking.*

But even in her demented state, she knew it was her own voice. She remembered Reeder ranting with his fever from the typhoid. *I hope the animals stay away. The bears and bobcats and…and rattlesnakes.* "Bears and bobcats and rattlesnakes!" she yelled. "Stay away from me! You just stay away from me!" She leaned back and pulled the blanket closer around her. The fire crackled; the owl continued to ask, "Whoo?" and the crickets sang and sang. Luvella's head spun, her heart galloped, and her body shook as she sank into a world of dark forests and dangerous animals and strange noises.

## Chapter Eleven

A hand touched her forehead. “Get away!” Luvella screamed. “I have to sleep,” she heard herself mumble. Her eyes still closed, she turned to her side. Pain knifed both her legs and her left arm. Her head throbbed. “Unhhh,” she groaned as she returned to her back.

She heard a soft step at her side. *Someone is here! I’m not dreaming!* She opened her eyes slowly. A pair of moccasins was at her side, raw deer hide trousers rising up from them. She gasped. *An Indian!*

Luke squatted beside her, his hand pressed to her forehead. Tiny beads in black, white, yellow and red trimmed his fringed shirt. A small dark leather pouch dangled from his neck on a strand of rawhide. “Luke! Oh, my goodness. I thought you were an Indian,” she said and, even in her semi-stupor, realized her hurtful mistake. *Mama’s right. Why don’t I think before I speak?*

Luke’s jawbone flexed, and the look of concern in his eyes shifted to a wounded indifference. “I am an Indian. I’m a Muncee. You knew that,” he said, his lips in a thin line, “but I thought it didn’t matter to you.” He stood and looked around. “We’ve got to get your fever down.” He picked up the white material beside Luvella’s ankle.

“No!” she said. “That’s…”

Luke looked at her, then opened the folds of

material to display Luvella's drawers. He grinned at her embarrassment.

As Luke walked toward the creek, Luvella shouted, "Luke Raven! Bring them back here!" The shouting exhausted her; she lay back and closed her eyes.

Luke worked quickly. He placed the cold, wet drawers on Luvella's head and stoked the fire. He made fresh poultice from her supply of snakeroot. He examined her broken ankle, touching it gently all around, just as Luvella had done. He nodded when he recognized where it was broken.

Then he took the drawers, turned them so the cold part was on the inside and wrapped them around her ankle. He filled her tin cup with water and set it on some hot coals. Opening the pouch hanging from his neck, he selected a tiny piece of lavender flower spike, rolled it back and forth between his hands until it formed a small pile of powder. He poured a drop of the warmed water from the tin cup into his palm and made a thick paste.

"This will heal that cut on your head." Luke dabbed it on her forehead. He made her some snakeroot tea and hand fed her some bread and apple butter.

"Now." He squatted in front of her. "We should get you home where you can get some real rest. But we already have a late start." He looked up at the sun, noon high. "You'll need some rest along the way. And"—he stood up—"we'll have to ride Daisy together."

Luvella looked at him, feeling a little more lucid. "Where's your horse?"

"I'll explain on the way. Right now, we have to break camp and get started to your Muncy Valley." He looked at her. "It may be spelled differently, but don't forget your village has the same name as my people." He spread apart the campfire coals and poured creek water on them. "And my people were here first."

"Oh, Luke, I'm sorry…" Luvella began.

Luke held up his hand. "Never mind, Luvella. Sometimes we show our true beliefs in simple mistakes."

He cleaned the campsite, took the saddle and blanket from behind Luvella, and prepared Daisy for travel. When everything was ready, he came over to the tree where Luvella sat.

"This will hurt, Luvella, but you have to stand before I can lift you onto Daisy. Here, let me do most of the work."

He bent down beside her and put an arm around her back and under her left arm. "Slowly now," he said, lifting her up. "Don't put any weight on your broken ankle. And just rest your other foot on the ground for balance. I've got you."

They stood like that, the two of them together, letting Luvella recover from the movement. The warmth of his breath flitted across her forehead, and his arm felt strong around her. *His arm is around me!*

"Are you all right?" He looked down at her.

Her throbbing ankle brought her back to her senses. Luvella clenched her teeth. "I'm fine. You don't have to treat me like a baby."

Luke threw his head back and laughed. "Good," he said. "Your old cantankerous self."

His voice softened. "This is the hard part, Luvella. I've got to get you up on Daisy. I'll try not to jar your ankle, but…" His voice trailed off as he lifted her onto the saddle. "Maybe you should ride side-saddle, and we can brace your leg out."

"I *hate* riding side-saddle," she retorted. "Besides we can hold my leg out in front of me riding regular. And the trail is narrow in some spots so that might be safer. My ankle will be closer to Daisy."

"Good thinking, Luvella. That tea must have really cleared your head."

He walked over to an ash tree and pulled down a rolled pack hanging from it. Luvella hadn't noticed it before. Thongs were tied around it and made a loop at one end. Luke poked his arm through the loop so the pack hung from his shoulder. He stopped at Daisy's side.

"Aha!" he declared. "I have the perfect arrangement for you."

He opened his pack—it was just a blanket wrapped around what looked like sticks. He arranged the blanket so it folded to about a very thick, soft foot square. The sticks turned out to be four short stakes, each the staff for an attached flag of material, and he placed them along her ankle for new braces. He wrapped the blanket around the braced ankle and used the untied thong to suspend her leg from around Daisy's neck. "This will keep the ankle from dangling and swelling." Luke arranged the saddlebags behind the saddle, and at last, he climbed onto the saddle behind Luvella.

His arms reached around her for the reins; she stiffened. "Don't worry, I won't hurt you, my pretty." He chuckled into Luvella's ear.

"Oh!" Luvella groaned her exasperation. "You are impossible."

Luke chuckled, deep in his throat. "*Tsch, tsch.*" He nudged Daisy with his heels.

Daisy settled in to a slow, even gait. Luvella winced and closed her eyes against the pain. But as she adjusted to Daisy's rhythm, the throbbing eased a little, and she relaxed. The blanket made an excellent cradle for her ankle and helped keep the braces tight.

"Now." Luke announced. "I will explain why I do not have a horse with me. I will also keep talking to you as we ride. You will have time to rest later, but please listen to me for a while. Thinking will help you stay awake—and fight the brainsickness."

He hesitated a minute. "First of all, the reason I am dressed like this—like an *Indian*," he emphasized, "is because I am on a vision quest."

"A vision quest?" Luvella echoed. Daisy's ears twitched. "I've never heard of such a thing."

Luke was silent a moment. Then he said, with a touch of sarcasm, "No, I'm sure you haven't. It's an Indian practice."

Luvella tried to turn in the saddle, but pain grabbed her ankle. "I said I was sorry, Luke. If you're going to keep punishing me for saying something I didn't mean, when I wasn't right in my head, you can just go off by yourself. I can get home—to Muncy Valley—perfectly well by myself." She was glad Luke couldn't see the tears threatening to spill down her cheeks. She really wanted to be in her soft bed, sleeping, with Mama there to take care of her.

"All right, Luvella. Truce." He adjusted his position, but his arms tightened to a firm hold on her. Her stomach grabbed.

"A vision quest is a…a search, a spiritual search. It is a tradition of all tribes, not just the Muncees. I have finished serving the white man by learning his ways all those years in that school. Now I must find *my* path in the world. I must learn the direction I should take for my future."

Luvella nodded. "That sounds…good, I guess. But what does that have to do with your horse, with your not having your horse?"

"I'm getting to that," he said. "Before you go on a vision quest, it's important that you pray—a lot. Your mind and your heart have to be clear, ready for the spirits to enter and to tell you your destiny. I was doing that before Aunt Hilda died." He hesitated a moment. "Once you've prepared thoroughly, then you set out on your journey." He shifted in the saddle slightly, and Luvella realized how uncomfortable he must be. He was giving her most of the saddle space.

He continued. "You select a place, deep in nature, where you feel close to the four directions. You set up your square, the place where you will stay until your vision comes to you. You use flags—those flags bracing your ankle—to mark the four directions around you. You shed your clothes and you stay there, naked, fasting and praying. It may be hours or, more likely, days before the spirits speak. So, you see, a horse would distract you and would not be happy fasting with you all that time."

"Hmmm," Luvella said. "Don't you burn from the day's sun and freeze at night without your clothes?" She could feel herself blush and wished she hadn't mentioned his being without clothes.

"You keep a blanket with you for protection; mine is around your ankle," Luke answered. "But when there is just you and the four directions and Mother Earth and the sun, you watch all the phases of nature. Often, your body isn't even aware of the heat or cold. You're fasting, so your mind becomes alert and focused. Then when you sleep, your dreams are very vivid and powerful. Usually, that's how the spirits speak to you—in your dreams."

He led Daisy off the trail toward a tree stump nearby. "This will make it easier for you to get off and back on Daisy." After jumping off the horse, he lifted Luvella carefully onto the stump and on down to the ground. She sat, leaning back against the stump.

The movement had activated the blood thumping in her ankle. Luvella pursed her lips together and silenced the groan that wanted to escape. Instead, she said between clenched teeth, "That's a beautiful ceremony. I've learned so much about the Muncee's ways lately. I feel like I'm almost Muncee myself. My mountain—North Mountain—is like a part of me. I talk to it all the time. And it talks to me, I think. Sort of like your spirits."

Luke looked at her quickly, his eyes a soft chestnut brown and questioning. But he said nothing. He took Daisy to the creek nearby to drink and brought water back for Luvella.

"Thank you," she said. "So what did the spirits tell you to do with your life?" She sipped the water from the same tin cup she'd had her tea in earlier.

"I found you before I found my special place. I have not had my vision yet."

Her head was beginning to ache, and she rubbed her forehead. Luke must have seen her motion and reached in a saddlebag for her drawers. This time Luvella let the groan slip. "You just love playing with my underdrawers, don't you?"

He grinned, turned to walk to the creek, and brought back her wet drawers, sashaying them back and forth and guffawing at Luvella's glare. She had never heard him laugh that hard before and was surprised at how deep it sounded. It reminded her of Uncle Isaac's rich voice.

He settled down, wrung the water from the drawers, and held them on her head for a few moments; then he wrapped them around her ankle. He mixed a fresh snakeroot poultice and tied it on the snakebite.

"We'll rest here for just a little longer," he said, looking skyward. "I'm afraid it will be nightfall before we reach your home."

Luvella rested against the stump and closed her eyes. *Oh, if I could just sleep.* Luke's hand slid back and forth on her forehead. So gentle, it barely touched her. She leaned her head into his hand, and he held it there. She dreamed she was riding Daisy in an open meadow, fast. The wind was whipping her hair and her clothes. She heard a sound, and there was Luke, riding a white stallion, beside her. He was smiling and reached his hand out to her.

A buzzing invaded her head; Daisy and Luke and his horse were gone. She tried to run but felt like she was sinking into a deep, dark hole. *Aunt Hilda's grave! No! No! I've got to get out of here!*

"Luvella!" Luke was shouting, his hand firmly grasping her shoulder.

She opened her eyes. She was sitting on the ground, *on top* of the ground. Luke let go of her shoulder and stood. "You were talking crazy," he said. "At least you slept a little. But we should really go." He frowned and stared down at her.

"Are you sure you can ride?" he asked. "We could camp here for the night and let you rest."

"I'm fine," she said, "and I'd really like to sleep in my own bed tonight."

The trail was smoother and easier now. Daisy could travel a little faster, and Luvella could still keep her rhythm without a lot of severe jostling. But the constant up and down motion was aggravating her ankle, and even the snake bite on her other leg. Fighting the pain took all her energy; it was her whole focus.

The sun had dipped behind the timberline. A crimson glow outlined everything. Her head fell forward; her eyes closed against the dizzying forest slipping by them. A drone in the distance lulled her into a reverie. Luke's arms tightened around her, pulling her upright. The drone was distinct now. Men's voices pierced the forest stillness.

"Are you awake, Luvella?" Luke whispered in her ear.

"Yes," she answered, although she wasn't sure.

"Indian!" a man shouted.

Luke held her even more tightly. "We're going to go a little faster, Luvella. Try to hang on." He urged Daisy on.

But not soon enough. "Injun! Injun!" men shouted. Luvella realized they had reached the tenant houses; they had gone beyond the road alongside Daddy's sawmill. A crowd of men had spilled into the yard from the tavern, located next to the houses. The smell of hard liquor hung in the warm evening air.

"Look at what that Injun done to that poor little girl," one man said.

A roar swelled. Men rushed toward them. *What's*

*happening? Why are they angry at us?* She held onto Daisy's mane, waiting to speed forward. But the men were all around them.

"Get him!" one said.

Then she felt Luke being yanked off the saddle. She winced as he slammed against the ground. The men were hitting him.

"Luvella! Go!" he yelled.

## Chapter Twelve

Daisy whinnied and pranced nervously. Luvella grabbed the reins and glided her hand soothingly over Daisy's chest. She squinted and forced her head into focus. She quickly searched the crowd—about eight or ten there. *Who are these men?*

A movement behind the crowd caught her attention. She saw a tall man, distinctive because of his natty clothes. Red hair peeked out from under his derby. As he moved, she saw his goatee. *Mr. Bocke. That was his voice that first shouted Indian.*

"Unnhhh." One of the men near her fell to the ground. *Luke was fighting back.* The sounds of knuckles hitting flesh made her head reel again. *Concentrate, Luvella.* She saw one of the men kick Luke. A rush of anger displaced her lightheadedness.

Then she remembered Daddy's words about her protection. She reached behind her into her saddlebag and pulled out the Colt. She pulled back the hammer on the gun and aimed it upward.

*Kabam!* The gunshot echoed from the mountain and filled the tavern yard with the sound of its explosion. The powder smell clung to the air and mingled with the rancid odor of spirits. The men stood still, suddenly silent. All eyes snapped to Luvella.

She aimed the gun just above their heads. "I have five shots left. If I hear even one gun cock, I'll shoot. If anyone moves, I'll shoot." The men still stood, still silent.

"Luke, get on." She nodded toward herself and the horse.

Luke sprung around from where he stood. For a few seconds, he glared at each of the four men surrounding him. Luvella noticed he was taller than two of the men. The sleeve of his deer hide shirt was torn from its shoulder seam. He turned his back to the men in a statement of defiance, and in an instant, he had jumped up on the horse.

Luvella clucked Daisy to turn around, clenching her teeth against the pain in her ankle. She kept the gun pointed at the men.

"Here," Luke said quietly to her. "I'll take the reins. You keep them at bay with the gun. But don't shoot."

Luvella smiled in spite of their situation. "I don't think I'll have to," she whispered. "I'm a crack shot, but they don't know that." She held the gun in a threatening aim, and the men stepped backward. "Our home is back a ways," she whispered to Luke. "Then turn right on the first road."

"Hold the thong to support your ankle, Luvella," Luke spoke softly, although his voice still had a deep timbre. "We are going to ride." He slapped the reins lightly against Daisy's side, and the horse sprung forward, as if even she knew the danger there.

They galloped down the road. Luvella clamped her lips together and closed her eyes, trying to think of anything other than the pounding throbs in her ankle. She felt Luke twist in his half of the saddle to look backward.

"They're getting on their horses." He urged Daisy to go even faster.

Luvella opened her eyes. "Oh! Take this road to Main Street. On that street, to the left a little, there's a short cut we can take to our house. Turn left there and then right.

"This is shorter and ends up right next to our property. It's an old log sluice and is pretty steep, though.

"There it is." She pointed to a barely discernible footpath from the road. "If we hurry up into the woods, they won't see us, and they'll go all the way to the mountain road."

Luke glanced backward again and led Daisy across the dried creek bed. On the other side, the trees greeted them. Luke slipped off the horse. "I'll catch up to you, Luvella, but you keep going. I want to make sure no one follows us here." He patted Daisy's rump firmly.

Luvella took the reins again, quietly urging Daisy up the steep incline. She was sure Luke had jumped off so Daisy could move more easily with just one rider. *Poor Daisy. You've had a hard day, too, haven't you?* The sluice had accumulated some rocks and ruts through the years of disuse, and the rough upward ride jolted Luvella's leg. She could *feel* her foot puff up, like Mama's bread rising. But the terror of the attack drove her onward. She pictured those men, hitting and kicking Luke.

*Luke. Where is he?* She reined Daisy in, turned as far as she could in the saddle, and searched the woods. "Luke," she whispered as loudly as she dared. "Luke. Are you out there? Are you safe?"

The woods were silent. It was dusk, and the

animals, sometimes smarter than humans, were burrowing in for the night. She thought she heard galloping horses continuing south of the railroad. *Good. They missed us.* She looked around her again. *Maybe they found Luke and are taking him somewhere.*

"Oh, Luke," she whimpered, one tear finding a trail down her cheek. "Don't let anything happen to you." She released a long, quivering sigh. "How can I go on when you could be in trouble?" She hung her head, closing her eyes to blink the tears away. Her exhaustion took over, and she just sat there, on Daisy, her shoulders shaking with silent sobs.

"Luvella," Luke said, coming from behind. "Are you hurt? Did something happen?"

She gulped her cries and wiped her face quickly with one hand, grateful for the cover of the evening shadows. "There you are!" She was angry, and it showed in her voice. "I thought those men had caught up with you. You could have let me know you were safe."

Luke frowned. "You are such a child sometimes. I never know what to expect from you."

"I am *not* a child. You're hardly any older than I am."

He walked in front of Daisy and pulled on the lead. "Come on, Girl, let's get going," he said to the horse. "I'll tell you how much older I am another time. I saw one man ride up that road, so he'll be coming up pretty soon. How far are we from your home?"

"Almost there." She turned to the task of getting up the mountain. "Daddy is probably out on the porch smoking his pipe right now." She thought of Mama in the kitchen and Daddy and her brothers. "It will be good to be home again."

Luke ran up the slope, and Daisy followed him. Luvella leaned onto Daisy's withers and reached down to help support her ankle. The pain was excruciating now. "Almost there," she whispered to herself. "Almost there almost there almost…"

They had reached the road. The sound of Daisy's hooves on the smooth dirt of the road was like a melody to Luvella. She sat up. "There!" She pointed to the left of the road. "See the lantern light through the windows? Our barn is just ahead."

"Ride! Go Luvella!" He slapped Daisy again. "And get inside your house as fast as possible. I'll cut through the woods and meet you there."

Luvella saw him run like wind into the forest toward her house. "*Tsch*, Daisy." She bent low to help Daisy gallop her final yards for this long day.

She was right. Daddy was on the porch. So was Jake. Reeder and Bill were in the yard, throwing their pig gut football back and forth. They all rushed to the drive as she reined in Daisy near the porch. Luke emerged from the woods and ran across the yard to her side, quickly lifting the thong from Luvella's ankle. He reached up for Luvella.

"Come on. I'll get you," he said.

Daddy and Bill stared first at Luke and then at Luvella's ankle. Reeder reached for Daisy's bit.

"Daisy's been rid hard. She's frothing," he said, his voice sharp with rebuke.

"That's the truth," Luvella commented. "This is Luke, Daddy. He's Uncle Isaac's nephew. Sort of saved my life."

Luke frowned at her again but barely nodding at

Daddy and her brothers. “There’s a man following us and should be coming up the road in a second or two.”

“He was with a bunch of men who attacked Luke,” Luvella added. “…unnhh. Easy with that ankle, Luke…”

Daddy took over. “Reeder, get Daisy in the barn and give her a good rubdown. Some extra oats, too. Luke, take Luvella into the house, and the two of you stay in there. Bill and Jake, come with me.” He carried his pipe and sauntered toward the end of their drive, where it meets the road. As Luke carried her through the door to the kitchen, Luvella could just barely see Daddy’s shadow lean against a tree next to the road and Bill’s and Jake’s on the other side of their drive, doing the same. Waiting. In the dark.

Inside, Mama rushed over as Luke brought Luvella in.

Luke nodded to Mama. “Mrs. Andersson, I’m Luke Raven, Isaac’s sister’s grandson. Luvella here has a broken ankle, and her other leg was bitten by a rattler.” Luke stood just inside the door, still carrying Luvella.

Luvella’s head lolled, as if it was too heavy for her to support.

Mama, whose face just blanched, put her hand on Luvella’s forehead. “She’s just a little feverish. Could you take her upstairs? Her room is just at the top of the stairs. I’ll be right up with a cold cloth.”

Mama bustled over to the sink as Luke carried Luvella to her room. He pushed open the door with his foot and placed her on her bed. When Luvella felt her bed under her, she forced her eyes open to prove to herself she wasn’t dreaming again. She still wasn’t sure, though, because there was Luke, staring down at her in her bedroom.

"Luke?" she murmured. "Are you really here?"

He smiled, just as Mama clumped into the room. Mama looked at Luke and then at Luvella and hesitated for just a second. "Here, Luvella. Let's put this on your head for a wee bit." Sitting on the bed, she put a damp cloth across Luvella's forehead. "Now. Tell me what you two have been up to."

Taking turns talking, the two of them related the story of Luvella's being thrown from Daisy and being bitten by the rattler and the struggle to keep her nausea and pain at bay.

Luvella finished, "I sort of dozed off on the last part of our ride home, so we went right past Daddy's road and all the way to the tavern. Some men yelled at us, pulled Luke off Daisy, and beat him. It was awful, Mama. If I didn't have Daddy's gun with me, Luke would surely be dead now."

"Gun?" Mama repeated. "How did you get your father's gun?"

Luke walked toward the door. "Mrs. Andersson, do you have some really cold water so we can put cold pads on Luvella's ankle? I think it has swollen a lot with our ride today."

Mama turned to examine the ankle, and Luke raised his eyebrows and flashed an 'I saved your life again' grin at Luvella. "Let me wet that cloth on her head again downstairs while you put something under her ankle to hold it up."

He grabbed the cloth and ran down the stairs. Luvella heard Daddy and Bill come into the kitchen, and Daddy's voice, all worried, ask, "How's Luvella?"

She couldn't hear Luke's answer.

He followed Daddy and Bill up the stairs to Luvella's room and handed the damp cloth to Mama. Mama had already removed the blanket and flags and had other blankets folded underneath Luvella's foot and leg. Her ankle looked like a young eggplant—ugly, purple, and very swollen.

Mama was clearly in charge. "Bill, will you get that bandage we used when you hurt your leg? And don't we have those braces from when Reeder broke his ankle? They're smooth and curved to fit the ankle. We have to get this ankle in place, or Luvella will never dance again." That was Mama's best attempt at a joke, and everyone chuckled. Even Luvella managed a smile.

"And Will." Mama looked hard at her husband. "I think Luvella will need a little of your whiskey to help her sleep tonight and kill that pain."

Daddy pretended to be shocked, but Mama was on a mission. "Just get some, Will. And then we'll talk about your gun."

Luvella noticed Luke's face as he saw Daddy, who had been fully in control down on the porch, change into a blushing-with-guilt mild-mannered servant. All at the hands, or the words, of this gentle, little woman. And her heart smiled.

Only minutes passed before Luvella had had some snakeroot tea, made by Luke with some of Daddy's "medicine" in it, a new brace applied over protective bandages, and a slice of Mama's bread, toasted on the stovetop, and slathered with Mama's apple butter.

"Oh, I am so glad to be home," Luvella said. She told her family how the snake had spooked Daisy and how she had passed that awful night in the woods alone. "If Uncle Isaac hadn't told me on our trip to his house how to treat snakebite, I could have died out there. That was a big snake." She closed her eyes, letting herself enjoy the soft bed and Mama's food inside her.

Luke told the rest of the story, but he stopped at the point when they reached the tavern. Luvella opened her eyes and looked at him. He looked downward, and Luvella saw him blushing. *He's embarrassed. I never thought about how he must feel to be hated so much.*

She continued, "There were men outside the tavern. You could smell the liquor all over. They saw my ankle braced and my head wrapped in a bandage, and they assumed Luke had done that to me. At least that's what they yelled." She finished the story and then remembered what else she had seen.

"Funny. Mr. Bocke was there, standing behind the men yelling at Luke, and I really think he started them going."

Bill exchanged looks with Daddy. "What?" Luvella looked from one to the other.

Daddy pulled at his mustache. "That man who had followed you rode right up to our drive and stopped. He was staring at the house when Bill and me stepped onto the road and surprised him. It was Sigfried Bocke. He said he was thinking of knocking on our door for directions. Claimed he'd taken the wrong road."

Bill said, "You should've seen his face when Daddy struck his match and started to light his pipe. I guess he hadn't seen us. Then we walked right up to him. For a minute, I thought he was gonna cry." Everyone laughed.

"I politely told him to turn around and go right back to where he came from," Daddy finished. Then he shook his head. "There sure is something strange about that man."

"By the by, Luvella," Reeder said. "When we went to the tavern the other night, just before you went to Forksville?"

Luvella nodded, already beginning to drowse.

"Well, we learned that Bocke and some other men are gambling and selling moonshine and planned to do that in the caboose and even Smythe's hotel."

"Not any more, though," Luvella managed. "The caboose is mine." She smiled, sleepily.

Mama sighed and slid off the bed to stand near Luvella.

"Shoo, all of you! Luvella has to sleep now, and I have to change her clothes. Luke, you can share Reeder's room, but first, Bill, fix him some dinner, will you?"

When they were gone, Luvella said, "Mama. I almost forgot, with everything that's happened. I have something for you—from Aunt Hilda."

Luvella closed her eyes as Mama washed the trail dust from her face and hands and helped her change into a nightgown. "And Mama, Aunt Hilda practically came back from the dead to give it to you. Remember that clothespin doll you made her?"

Mama stopped her ministrations and sat up straight. Her eyes, suddenly rimmed in red, watered. She whispered, "Aunt Hilda still has that doll?"

Luvella's breathing was soft. She barely murmured, "*Mm-hmm*. It's in my saddlebag. Hannah, that's Luke's sister, and Uncle Isaac said Aunt Hilda had held something real tight in her one hand for days." Luvella held one hand in a tight fist to show Mama.

"Aunt Hilda was so still, Mama, when I walked into her room. She looked dead already." Mama let a small gasp escape, and Luvella patted her hand. "But when I told her who I was…" Luvella had to swallow to steady her voice. "…Mama, she woke right up and started talking. We couldn't understand her words, but she held my hands and gave me that doll. She thought I was you, Mama. Then she went right back to her deep, deep sleep."

Luvella could say no more. That wondrous moment with Aunt Hilda, the nightmarish accident, and drama-filled ride home, and the whiskey-augmented tea helped release her thus far repressed emotions. A deluge of tears ran down her face, and one loud sob escaped.

Mama's face flushed as her eyes filled. She patted Luvella's hand and brushed her daughter's tears from her face.

"Thank you for going to Aunt Hilda for me," she said softly. "It…it meant a lot to both of us." Then Mama turned to reach for something.

The cold sliver of scissors slid up Luvella's leg as Mama cut, then pulled, the drawers off her, and Luvella knew Mama was being careful to cut on the seams so they'd be easy to re-stitch. She felt Mama's light kiss on her forehead, heard her pick up the lantern, and close the door behind her.

She heard her own breathing, deep and rhythmic. She slept…and slept.

## Chapter Thirteen

When she awoke, her leg muscles were tight, but no pain shot up from the snake-bitten area. *I won't wiggle my toes just yet,* she joked to herself.

Luvella lifted herself to her elbows. *Ohhhh, my poor muscles. They'll remind me all day of my long ride yesterday, on top of my adventure in the woods.* Carefully—very carefully—she inched to the edge of her bed, using both hands to pull her left leg with her and lift it down to the floor. Her foot felt as if it were steeped in mud, but she sat up and looked around her room. Propped against the wall, right next to her bed, were crutches! She recognized Reeder's handiwork immediately.

*Reeder, you are either a devil or an angel. This is definitely your angel work.* She used them to pull herself to a standing position and practiced using them to walk around her room, stopping at her window. "There you are, my beautiful mountain. I'm back. Have you missed me? We have much work to do, you know. My store, the basket bonanza…"

A reflection from the creek caught her attention, and she looked down. A man was there—in the water. His back, broad and muscular and *naked,* was turned toward her. "One of those men from last night!" she said aloud. Just as she was about to call Daddy, the man plunged under the water, twisted around, and jumped up, facing her. He shook the water off his hair and began his climb from the creek.

"Oh Glory! It's Luke." Luvella turned her face away just in time to avoid seeing his emerging body. "Oh my." She pressed her hands on her suddenly hot cheeks. A little breathless, she clumped over to her washstand, rested lightly on her right leg while leaning heavily on the crutches and began to wash up. She splashed water on her face, then held the soaked washcloth to her face and neck. She felt so warm. She stood and studied her reflection in the looking glass, wrinkled her nose, and stuck her tongue out at the sight of her hair. "Who is this wild Indian staring at me?"

Realization struck her fast as a rattler's bite. *Oh, Luvella. What poison you spew.* She thought of beautiful Hannah, of wise Uncle Isaac, and quiet, thoughtful Luke.

A knock on her door startled her. "Luvella, I have your clean drawers here—the ones cut to fit over your ankle. Do you need help getting dressed?"

"Come in, Mama, I'm managing. Thank you for washing them." She grinned at Mama's look of relief when she saw her daughter bright and bristly again. "I'm starving. Is that your sausage I smell cooking?"

Mama was already going back down. "Yes, but that's for the men. I think you should have a little porridge until your stomach is all settled."

As Luvella closed her door, she heard Reeder outside yell, "Now that you're all pretty, Luke, wanna throw some passes till breakfast?" Luke and her brothers all laughed, and there were grunts and heavy shuffles in the yard. "Football," Luvella grumbled, shaking her head.

Finally, she was dressed, had her hair pulled back with a large bow, and struggled down the stairs to the table.

Luke, in the kitchen now, followed her with his eyes. “Do you need help on the stairs, Luvella?”

Reeder said, “We could toss you down. It would be a lot faster.” Then he guffawed. Bill and Jake smirked a little, and Luke looked from one to the other.

Luvella retorted, “I hope when you’re playing football that you remember Luke was almost killed last night, and I’m sure is plenty sore.”

“That’s enough,” Mama said, and everyone was quiet. She placed a small bowl of porridge in front of Luvella.

“Mama,” Luvella whined. “I lo-ove your sausages. And I am soooo hungry.”

Mama got a plate and put it in front of Luvella. “Just a taste, or you’ll pay the price later.”

“You should listen to your mother,” Luke said. “She’s right.”

With that, Luvella stabbed two large sausages from the platter and a flapjack. She poured gobs of Mama’s maple syrup over the flapjack and started eating like a starving logger, cutting off large portions and chewing voraciously.

When she was finished, she smacked her lips and looked at Luke with a cocky smile of satisfaction. Then to Daddy, she said, “How are the preparations going for our festival? Is everyone working on it?”

“Well, I don’t know how the ladies are doing. Ben Smythe is still worried about Bocke taking over his hotel. That guy keeps hanging around everywhere.” Daddy frowned. “Last night, I let him know he wasn’t welcome up here, and that was before I knew what he'd been up to."

Luvella drummed her fingers on the table, rapidly at first, then more and more slowly as her face brightened with inspiration. "Mama, would you mind if we held a meeting here tomorrow morning? I think we have enough room for everybody. Today, I want to check on my store sales and then look over the caboose, but I think after that my ankle will want to stay right here to home." She looked at Daddy. "I think it's good to not let Mr. Bocke know about our meeting."

Luke got up from the table. "I'll let you people talk. I have to get ready for my hike back."

"Oh, Luke. Stay for a few days." Luvella could feel everyone's eyes focused on her. "You can get to know my family—we're Aunt Hilda's family, too—and I'd really like to show you my store." She sensed, rather than saw, Mama's discomfort.

But after only a moment's hesitation, Mama added, "Reeder can lend you one of his outfits to wear around here while I mend that sleeve for you. We'd be proud to have one of Isaac's family stay with us for a spell."

*Oh my goodness.* Luvella thought. *I forgot. He's an Ind... He's a Muncee. He could never walk into town with those vision quest clothes he's wearing.*

Luke hesitated, looking at the faces turned toward him. "I could stay another night. Thank you. Then I must go." He opened the door and called back. "Reeder, can I toss a few with your football?"

Reeder waved Luke a yes as Luvella felt Mama's gaze and the heat rising up to her face. Her stomach was making ominous sounds and beginning to churn. She ignored all this. She had things to do. But shaking her head, she said, "He must love football like you, Reeder. Those men last night were really beating him, and one kicked him when Luke was on the ground."

"Those are rough men there, Luvella," Reeder said. "We've played football against them, and they fight mean and dirty." Bill and Jake agreed.

Daddy nodded. "And our Mr. Bocke does seem to have a knack at riling people. But Luvella, Luke *is* an Indian, that's a fact." He stared right at her, hard.

"He's only half Indian. His mother is white." Her stomach flipped around dangerously. Nausea was directly under one of those flips, pushing bitter bile up into her mouth.

"Oh my! I have to get to the privy," she said, grabbing her crutches.

Reeder held the door open. "Hurry up, Luvella. Not in here."

She got halfway to the privy and had to vomit on the grass, right in front of Luke, who was tossing Reeder's football up in the air and catching it. She bent over as far as she could while still hanging onto the crutches, and retched…and retched. Luke threw the ball to Reeder and disappeared, but came back to her with a wet cloth. She used it to wipe her face and mouth.

He shook his head. "Your mother told you to go easy on the food. Don't you *ever* listen to what other people say?"

Luvella turned around clumsily. "I'm fine, Mr. Know-it-all. I'm just fine, thank you very much."

She stormed back to the house as sedately as the crutches and broken ankle would allow. Reeder was already throwing buckets of creek water on the mess she had left on the grass. She could hear him groan with every bucket.

Inside, Daddy was still at the table, sipping his coffee. Mama was boiling water and asked, "Do you have any more of those snakeroot leaves, Luvella? That tea settled your stomach pronto last night."

"Why yes, Mama. Here, right in my saddle bag."

Daddy was pulling at his mustache, which meant he was thinking. "Luvella, we'll go around today and tell each person ourselves about the meeting tomorrow morning. You tell Steckie and Ben Smythe—I'll have Bill and Reeder send them to you—and they and I will do the rest. That way, Mr. Bocke won't know about it. If someone—like Ben Smythe—happens to mention it to him, then so be it. If he comes, so be it."

He pinched his brows together. "But besides checking on the progress, we also have to let these people know where the baskets are coming from. Isaac and others will be bringing those baskets here. We don't want any ruckus like last night's." He looked at her, like he had a few moments ago, peering through her eyes into her soul. "I'll handle that part of the meeting. You do the rest."

He stood, slapping his hands on the table. "Better get started on our day. Margaret, are you feeling up to cleaning this mess?" He looked at Mama, who beamed under his concern.

"Ah yes." She waved him away. "I feel real good now, real good." She smiled. Luvella smiled too. She had noticed how Mama's color and breathing were regular. Her health had definitely improved in the last week.

"Thanks for the tea, Mama. It was just right," Luvella whispered. She didn't want Luke to hear, wherever he was.

Outside, Daddy took Luvella and Luke, wearing Reeder's shirt and trousers, in the wagon while Bill and Reeder rode the other two horses, falling in behind the wagon. Jake had already gone to the sawmill.

Reeder said, "Luke, you handle that football like a real quarterback. Have you played much?"

Luke grinned. "I just finished my fourth year on Carlisle Industrial's team."

When the silence was so "loud" and long, Luvella turned to look at her brothers. They both were staring at Luke, mouths open. Finally, Bill said, "You mean…with Jim Thorpe?"

Luke nodded. "Ayup. I lived, ate, and played with Jim. Of course, right now he's on his way to Stockholm for the Olympics."

Reeder brought his horse alongside the wagon. "You're the linebacker Luke Raven we always hear about?"

"That's me." Luke blushed at Reeder's stare.

Bill said, "I knew your name was the same, but I just never…"

Luke nodded. "I love playing football, love winning at football, but I really want to be a doctor. When we weren't practicing or playing, I worked at Carlisle's infirmary. Got pretty good at it, Dr. Rogers said. He's the school's doctor."

The conversation stopped there, and everyone rode quietly down the mountain road. In town, Daddy said, "Wanna look in on your caboose first, Luvella?"

It was strange how Daddy and her brothers were grinning, as if they were enjoying some private joke.

She was still annoyed at Luke for acting like he

was so much more grown up than she was, but she couldn't hide her excitement about her future little store. "Luke, it's a mess right now. You just have to use your imagination when you see the inside."

Daddy lifted her down from the wagon and led her up the five steps to the caboose. He fumbled with the door and pushed it open finally, stepping inside. There, he stood back and let Luvella in.

Her head was down, watching her crutches so as not to fall over the threshold. When she looked up, she stopped moving, stood absolutely still. She opened her mouth to speak, but her voice wouldn't come out. She couldn't absorb everything in front of her, process it into her head, it was so completely different from how she'd left it.

Everything was new and shiny. Her gifts were there, displayed on tables and in one shelved cabinet with a glass top and front. The walls were freshly painted in pale lavender. The stove was scrubbed back to its original silver color, and when she opened its door, she saw a small pile of firewood ready for her first fire. And there were gifts she'd never seen before, obviously new consignments. *I'll have to record those items and talk to the owners about prices.*

"So, what d'ya think, Sis?" Reeder had pushed his way in and around her. "We moved the desk to the back, at Bessie's suggestion, polished the top of it, and got it looking just like new. Bessie put your record books there, and there are drawers underneath for your cash box and other things. Bessie also brought your stuff over from Steckie's and arranged it here."

Luvella squealed and lunged at Reeder with her arms open. Hugging him, she said into his shirt, "Oh, thank you. Thank you." She leaned back on her crutches and thanked Daddy and Bill, both still grinning. "Oh, I never dreamed cleaning this up would be so easy," she said, and the men all laughed. Even Luke.

She looked around the caboose, savoring every sparkling window, the deep burgundy hue of the polished desk, every lilac curtain—a shade darker than the lavender paint and obviously Mama's handiwork—at the windows. "This is truly beautiful," she whispered, her eyes wet. "Thank you."

Daddy winked at her. "Reeder, you run over to the hotel now and ask Mr. Smythe to come see Luvella. Bill, you go ask Steckie. Then we'll stop at the others' on our way to the mill."

Daddy was trying to keep her from being on her feet too much, but he was also trying to keep Luke from being seen. *How can I get these people to open their minds and hearts when I say stupid things myself like 'wild Indian'?*

Daddy said, "One last thing. There are new keys for the doors. I just put them on the desk over there. For some reason, Lars wanted me to make sure you know there are new locks on both doors."

Luvella remembered the moonshine jugs in the stove, but she didn't mention it now.

"We'll leave the wagon for you and Luke to take back home. Don't let her stay here too long, Luke."

Luke grinned down at her. "I won't," he answered her father. And then, quietly, to her, "That makes me boss, doesn't it?"

"Oohhh!" She shook her head, clenching her fists, and turned away from him. But she could feel his uneasiness, his uncertainty. And her own.

*What will our friends think about our Indians? What will they do?*

## Chapter Fourteen

The next morning, feeling much like her former self, she prepared for her day. Checking discreetly at her bedroom window, she saw Luke fully in the water and splashing his face and hair, rubbing them.

*He's washed in the creek two days in a row. Is this part of his vision quest? Or does he jump in the creek every day?*

She moved to one side of the window, so Luke was out of her sight, but she could still see her mountain. She thought about her time with Luke yesterday and didn't resist letting her lips turn up in a smile. *He makes me so mad sometimes, but I feel…like I'm on top of my mountain when I'm with him. Like the whole world is there, just for us.*

Still smiling, she looked out at her mountain. "Thank you for bringing me back safely…finally…from Aunt Hilda's. Now we have much to do, you know. Are you ready to help me? To inspire me? Especially about bringing the Indians here?" She searched the towering mountain, the sea-green, the apple-green and moss-green of its leafy trees and the deep blue sky above them. She felt the beauty of it all, the deep sense of peace it always brought to her. She pressed her hand to her heart, as if to hold it inside her, to bring the heartbeat of the mountain in with her own.

A ray of sun glittered through the forest, like a tiny angel on a mission. She remembered Uncle Isaac speaking to her as they rested on their trip up the mountain. She had been feeling very efficient, telling him more about the Basket Bonanza and her business goals.

"Luvella," he had said, his voice resonating, like the organ in church. "It sounds like you know what you want, but to really achieve it, you must become the goal."

She had asked him, "How can I become my goal? Especially when there are so many pitfalls in my path?"

He smiled. "You are already a leader. That is good. But you must lead with heart. Find your people's strengths and nurture them; develop a vision instead of plans; and keep your principles and honesty in everything."

She blinked at her mountain. "Have I been completely honest with the other merchants?"

She thought of Luke now and how uncomfortable both Steckie and Mr. Smythe had been with him yesterday. They were both polite, though, which left a little hope in the corner of her heart. Anna, on the other hand, was busting at the seams, her eyes, sparkling with questions and insinuations, darting from Luke to Luvella to Luke. Anna would bombard her with questions when they were alone together today.

"Oh Glory!" Luvella's hand came up to cover her mouth. "Oh my! Luke is going back today." She clenched her hands together and implored her mountain, "Please don't tell me I'll never see him again."

She turned and thumped down the stairs as quickly

as the crutches would allow.

Luke, wearing his Indian suit Mama had repaired, was at the table with Bill and Reeder. Mama had just gone to the stove to get warm porridge for Luvella, who smiled at her mother and said, “Why thank you, Mama. And I can get my own food now, so you just sit down.”

She poured a generous amount of maple syrup over the porridge and some milk from the pitchers on the table, feeling Luke’s eyes watching her. She felt like saying to him, “See? I do listen to people sometimes.” But she continued her breakfast preparations meticulously.

When Daddy came in from outside, she said, “Good morning. Are we ready for our meeting?” She looked at her father, still ignoring Luke.

“I’m ready, but still thinking. This will be a tough one.” Then Daddy saved her from an awkward question to Luke. “Luke, are you sure you want to leave us today? You are welcome in our home, you know.”

Luvella finally looked at Luke. He cleared his throat. “Thank you, Mr. Andersson. But I have to be on my way. The only reason my family hasn’t been out looking for me is because they know a vision quest can take up to two weeks sometimes.”

At Luvella’s prodding, Luke had explained the ceremony to her family last night. However, he had begun his explanation by saying, “I should have told you, Luvella, the United States forbids my people to perform any of our ceremonies. So, it would be very dangerous for me, probably a prison sentence, if any of you mentioned this to anyone else.” Then, showing his trust, he told her family about the tradition of vision quest.

He stood now and carried his dishes to the sink. "I have a long walk today." He grinned. "I should leave right now."

"Reeder could take you on horseback to the other side of my sawmill. Give you a head start," Daddy said. He didn't say, "and protect you from those thugs who might still be loitering around the tenant houses."

Luke blushed, showing he understood the unspoken words. "I am better on foot. No one will see me this way." He picked up his blanket roll by the door and looped the thong over his shoulder.

Luvella's heart dropped abruptly to her stomach and lodged there. *How can I say goodbye to him?*

"Next time you're here, Luke, we'll have a football game," Reeder called. Luke grinned and waved.

"Luvella, why don't you go out and point him in the right direction?" Daddy said.

She looked quickly at Daddy, grateful that he didn't give her his usual wink. Everyone stood and wished Luke a safe journey and good vision quest and then Luke and Luvella were outside.

They walked to the road, slowly because of Luvella's crutches. Both were silent. Luvella wondered if all sorts of words were piling up in Luke's head like they were in hers. And still she said nothing.

They stopped, side by side, at the edge of her drive, at the edge of the road. Luke turned to face her. Luvella could see him struggling for the right way to say…what he wanted to say.

"Luvella," he began, studying the texture of the dirt road. "Your people and my people, they aren't really that different. But they do not blend well." He looked at her, his eyes dark and sad. "At least, I do not see the white man happy to make our acquaintance."

Luvella quelled the knot in her stomach, the tears pushing to fill her eyes. *What is he saying? Is this goodbye—forever? Is he saying we can never see each other again?*

She took a deep breath. "Luke, except for those wildcats at the tavern the other night, I thought the white man, as you put it, was quite nice to you. Mr. Smythe is stuffy with everyone new to town, and my family certainly likes you. I hope you can see that."

She turned intense eyes up to him, wanting him to like her friends, wanting him to like being here.

For just a second, he was uncertain. Then he smirked and said, "Your family was just grateful to me that I saved your life and dragged you home safely." He laughed his deep, Uncle-Isaac-baritone laugh.

"Oohhh, you…" she growled, clenching her fists. He was always making her mad like that. She raised her right fist as if to hit his shoulder, but he caught her wrist. He held it in the air a moment, still chuckling. Then his eyes grew sad again. No, more like wistful. He let her wrist down and slid his hand around her hand, squeezing it ever so slightly.

"I think you will interfere with my vision quest," he said softly. "I will miss you, Luvella."

He let go of her hand and turned toward the old sluice shortcut.

"Luke!" she called, unable to keep the warble from her voice or the tears from her eyes. He kept going, waving one hand in farewell without turning.

"Goodbye, Luke Raven!" she cried. "Goodbye." She was sobbing, and she didn't care if he heard her. She stood there, watching him go down the road and disappear into the woods. She stood there, waiting for him to come back.

## Chapter Fifteen

Luke didn't come back. She wiped her face with her hands, trying to remove the trace of tears before she rejoined her family. She hobbled back up the drive, stopped at the well, and splashed her face with some of its cold water. Then she continued to the privy, where she could sit privately and get ready for her life—her white man's life.

When Luvella re-entered the house, she frowned, forcing her control. Remembering the meeting, for which the folks should start arriving soon, helped her focus. She also reminded herself of her caboose, and how she had to re-organize her merchandise and her records, and decide what her new store sign should say. Her brothers had done a great job when they moved everything, but she knew exactly how she wanted her things to be displayed.

She was thinking again. Her head was working; her heart was subdued; her stomach was normal. Well, almost.

Bill and Jake were saddling up to go to the sawmill. It had been agreed that, after the meeting, Daddy would take Luvella in the wagon and leave her at her store. They would continue this routine until her ankle healed. Reeder would ride with them, too, except today he walked to the sawmill because of the meeting. Luvella helped Mama clean up the breakfast dishes.

"We had so much more room in our other house," Mama worried.

Luvella hardly ever thought of the home she grew up in, the home they had lost when Daddy and her brothers were struggling to survive the typhoid and couldn't work. She hadn't realized how much Mama must miss it, must miss the soundness of its construction and the grandeur of the two parlors and large kitchen. Mama never complained, so Luvella was surprised to learn her mother was concerned about what people would think about their home now.

"Mama, don't you fret," Luvella soothed. "These are hard-working folk, coming to get some work done. This is much better than sitting in our drafty church."

Daddy, sitting at the table, looked over toward the sink. "Margaret, you've turned this house into a palace. But I'll get you a nicer one some day." When Mama started to say something apologetic, he put up his hand. "It's a good plan to have these folks here today. They'll be in my home, and because of that, I think they'll pay more attention to what I have to say."

Luvella stopped drying the dish in her hand and looked at Daddy. "You are a fox!" She chuckled, and he tried to control the grin spreading across his face.

Luvella barely had time to arrange her festival records on the kitchen table before the people started coming in. Steckie was first; Mrs. Maarten and Mrs. Kiergen came up together; Mr. Melk, the farrier, and Mr. Pearson, the country storeowner, came in next, followed by Mr. Johannson, who handed a lease for Luvella to sign, then Mr. Smythe and finally, Mr. Harley, the banker.

Luvella immediately read the simple letter, leasing

the caboose to her for just six months and handed it to Daddy to read. When he nodded approval, she signed it and handed it back to Mr. Johannson. "Only six months?" she asked him, her brows wrinkling together.

"Sorry, Luvella," he answered. "The railroad wants to honor your proposal to rent, first, but then wants to have the caboose available for a possible sale." He shrugged and sat down.

Luvella waved the lease in front of everyone there. "This paper means my crafts' business is officially living in the caboose. Now you can stop in and see all the work my parents and brothers did to get it in good repair."

With congratulations being sent from around the table, she smiled and sat at the head, glancing at Steckie.

Steckie, who usually began the town meetings, spoke from his chair. "Luvella, this festival is your bailiwick. You lead the way today."

Luvella smiled a brief thank you, then still sitting, looked at everyone. "First of all, I want to apologize for being gone all week, but…"

"Uhh, Luvella, I'll take care of that later." Daddy spoke up, giving her a "let this one go" look.

She dipped her pen into the inkwell in front of her. "All right. Ummm, let's start with you, Mrs. Maarten. How are your plans coming along?"

Thirza Maarten stood, looked down at the paper in her hands, and blushed a little. Luvella realized this is the first time she'd seen Mrs. Maarten speak at the group's meeting. "Mr. Smythe has kindly offered to rope off a twelve by twelve area in front of his inn for us to set up a table and sell picnic lunches. We'll have those two long tables Mr. Andersson had built for our other picnics. I have seven young ladies who have promised delicious lunch baskets for nice, hungry young men."

Everyone laughed, even Mrs. Maarten. "If we can get some large baskets, I'd like to have some women put together picnic baskets for families. Of course, we would need all our baskets a week or two before the," she hesitated, "the bonanza." She smiled, as if in triumph. "You can put that in your advertising, Luvella. Maybe encourage people to come from nearby towns, like Forksville and Eagles Mere and even Dushore."

Luvella widened her eyes and smiled her excitement, not wanting to interrupt Mrs. Maarten. The woman, bolstered by the approving murmurs in the room, continued, "Mrs. Kiergen has met with Mr. Smythe, and they've decided to have chicken and a roast pig—Mr. Melk will sell one of his pigs to us for half price." There were more murmurs and nods. "Mr. Smythe will have lots of potatoes and coleslaw at the inn. And I have a list of people who will bring loaves of bread and pies for dessert."

Mrs. Kiergen whispered something to Mrs. Maarten. "Oh yes," Mrs. Maarten added. "We can put prices on our picnic baskets when we know what the baskets will cost us." She sat down.

Luvella was writing as fast as the pen would scratch across the paper, dipping it into the inkwell at intervals. She looked up. "Remarkable job! The three of you! Next, Mr. Smythe."

The reports continued. Luvella told them all of her pride in their dedication, cooperation, and especially in their results. "Thank you all for our vision," she added to herself.

"I've seen samples of the baskets we'll be getting and they're beautiful. Very well made. The price range is ten cents for very small, like for my soaps, twenty-five cents for the other small ones up to fifty cents for the largest ones—for your family size picnic lunch. We can charge double their prices, easily. I'll have a better idea of how many they can provide us in a few weeks."

"Anything else?" She looked at the faces looking at her.

Mr. Smythe stood, turning his hat round and round in his hands. "I'm making plans for this here festival, but Mr. Bocke really wants to have me turn the hotel over to him. He's got the money, he says, and Mr. Harley keeps asking me to pay the bank money I haven't got."

Whispers and mumbling and shuffling of feet permeated the room. Mr. Harley, protruding his chin and scratching his neck, coughed, as if something were stuck in his throat.

Daddy stood. "If you're done, Luvella, I'll take over." She nodded and sat down.

"Mr. Harley…Jude," Daddy looked directly at him. "Could the bank relax its rules a few more weeks until after the festival? If that doesn't bring the hotel back to solvency, then I'd be willing to help Ben out. Anyone else here willing to loan Ben some money later on to tide the inn for a couple months?"

Mr. Pearson, Mr. Johannson, and Mr. Melk quickly replied with 'Ayups' and raised hands.

Daddy had more to say. "Now, something's been bothering me all along about Mr. Bocke. Does anyone know anything about him?" Daddy looked around at all the shaking heads. "Ben, do you know where he's from?"

Mr. Smythe said, "No, Will. He's never said. He just asks questions and tells me he can't wait much longer, that he'll spend his money elsewhere."

Daddy tweaked his mustache. "He was actually spying on this house the other night. I'd sure like to know where he came from and what he's about."

Mr. Johannson raised his hand. "Will, d'ya want me to send some inquiries out on the telegraph? At least to the bigger towns near here, like Dushore and Williamsport? I don't like his always nosing around, either. And the railroad wants some proof that he's able to actually buy the caboose and its land before they take it away from Luvella here."

The women gasped and all eyes turned on Luvella. "I'm fine for a while," she said, and held up her lease.

Daddy pointed his finger at Mr. Johannson. "Excellent idea about checking on him, Lars. He's not the only one who can snoop." Everyone chuckled.

"Now," Daddy said. "Luvella, I have all the toothpicks the world will ever need, ready and waiting for the festival. And a place in front of the sawmill to set up some baskets for sale." He walked away from Luvella a little and faced the people.

"Margaret's aunt took sick a while back and was…on her last legs. Her husband came here to ask Margaret to take care of her during her last days. Margaret couldn't, so Luvella went in her place. Luvella has told us how the family and neighbors were really kind to her and how they were there every day to help with Aunt Hilda and guide Luvella in what to do. When Hilda died, they were there all day and into the night, taking over for Luvella."

Everyone nodded their heads and smiled at Luvella. Murmurs of "That's nice" and "How thoughtful" floated in the air.

"The fact is," Daddy said, "Hilda's husband, Isaac, is a Muncee Indian, and so are several of the people who helped Luvella and were so nice to her." He looked each person, one by one, in the eye. "And they are the same people who will be weaving the baskets for our festival."

Now the whispers multiplied and sounded like the beginnings of a dust storm. Daddy waited a moment.

"There's something else," he said, and immediately had everyone's attention again. "Luvella insisted to her Uncle Isaac that she could ride back here to Muncy Valley alone. So when a rattler spooked her horse, which threw Luvella to the ground and broke her ankle, she was alone in the woods. The rattler also bit her on the other leg, so she was in bad trouble."

Everyone looked at Luvella's braced ankle.

"Now, Steckie and Ben, you both met Luke yesterday. He's Isaac's sister's grandson, just returned home from the U.S. boarding school in Carlisle. He was hunting in the woods and found Luvella there. He told us that she had taken good care of both her legs, but she was feverish and delirious from the snake bite."

Mr. Johannson interjected, "Luvella, you're the only girl I know who coulda survived that!"

Everyone laughed. "Ayup. Ayup."

Daddy smiled, too. "Luke helped her get home safely. He's a good lad, smarter than most of us, has had more schoolin' than us, too, and, as it turned out, he put his life in danger for Luvella's sake."

There wasn't a sound in the room. Everyone stared at her father, waiting for what would come next.

"Luvella had dozed off on the last leg of their trip here, so they overshot their turn. They came to the tenant houses, and I guess the hot weather brought some men outside in front of the tavern. One man called out 'Indian,' and the rest took over. They attacked and beat Luke. He told Luvella to ride away and leave him there."

When Daddy hesitated, Steckie asked, "What happened then?"

"Well, Luvella had my Colt and when she fired it, everybody stopped."

The men in the room guffawed. "Luvella coulda fixed them good." "Did you show 'em your blue ribbons, Luvella?"

Luvella lowered her head and smiled.

Daddy added, "Luvella held them at gunpoint as she and Luke galloped off. She led Luke to the shortcut up the mountain here and the men chasing them missed that and then gave up the chase."

Daddy paced again. "Except for one man." He looked at Mr. Smythe. "Our Mr. Bocke. He came up the road and right to our house."

The people muttered to each other and shifted in their chairs.

"Here's the thing," Daddy said. Luvella knew this would be his punch point. "Margaret and her whole family shunned Hilda for marrying an Indian. Now Hilda's dead, and we can never make that up to her. Margaret feels awful about that.

"But we, here in Muncy Valley, which, by the way, is named after the Muncee Indians, we here in Muncy

Valley can show the world that we are good neighbors and live by the golden rule. We can buy the Indians' baskets and sell them—helping both us and them. And we can welcome them into our village and into our festival."

Daddy let out a long sigh. "We can all profit from that!" He waited a second and then sat.

Silence! Luvella thought of how quiet the world is just before a wicked storm. She waited. And waited. *Would there be a wicked storm here in Mama's house?* Finally, she was about to end the meeting, but was thinking of what to say.

Steckie spoke up. "I met Luke yesterday, and he seemed like a regular sort. He sure took good care of my little sister-in-law. But I was wondering, Will. What if some ornery types get wily at the festival? Like those ones at the tenant houses? What will we do?"

Mr. Melk said in his husky voice, "Ve could sic Luvella on dem."

The laughter cleared the tension for a welcome second. Then silence hung in the air again. Luvella thought of Luke, how those men had hit and kicked him, yet he was concerned only for her safety. She thought of Hannah, and Uncle Isaac and Mrs. Raven and the others, all quiet, gentle people who welcomed her into their circle.

Still no one spoke. The heat rose in Luvella, to her neck, to her face. *Why couldn't at least one other person speak up, say yes! We will open our town to them. We will eat with them...* Still, there was silence. *Does that mean that Luke will never be able to come here?*

She stood up, rage belching poison arrows from her

eyes. She saw Daddy, out her corner vision, looking at her, his own eyes wide with his sense of impending disaster. She gathered her papers, her pen and inkwell, slowly, purposefully, as she picked her words.

"Since you don't want to let my friends from the Muncee tribe into our town, we won't have baskets to sell. We won't have a basket bonanza without the baskets. And you won't have me to help you anymore." She looked every single one of them in the eye.

"This meeting is over," she said softly. She turned her back on them and thudded up the stairs to her room. Any place to be away from them!

"Luvella! Luvella!" Mr. Smythe was on his feet, gesturing with his arm. "C'mon now, Luvella. Don't be like that."

Luvella hurried up the steps and closed her bedroom door behind her. She could hear Mr. Smythe pleading to Daddy to beg her to reconsider, to be in charge of the festival. "It doesn't have to be a basket bonanza," he said. Others were talking, too, everyone to each other. Then a quiet settled over them.

Daddy's voice was loud. Luvella was sure he wanted her to hear him. He said, "This was Luvella's meeting. You heard her. The meeting's over, and I think you've all made a terrible mistake. Now that there is no festival."

## Chapter Sixteen

The ride into town was quiet. Luvella fixed her vision on the wagon wheel tracks on the road before them, usually devoid of heavy traffic markings this far up. Their house was the highest up the road, even though it was only half way up the mountain. Her father, concentrating on driving the wagon, uttered a kind word to the horse every little while.

In front of the caboose, Daddy helped Luvella down from the wagon. "Will you be all right today? First whole day all alone here." He peered at her.

"I'm fine, thank you. I'll be fine."

But she wasn't so sure. She unlocked her door, the first time for her, and entered her caboose. Yesterday, Luke had been with her. She had felt such pride as she showed him all the things she had for sale, and then the beauty of the caboose itself, thanks to her father and brothers. Now…she looked around, trying to lift her mood, to shove aside the feeling of doom that had enveloped her back home. She picked up a sweater from a tabletop and replaced it without examining it.

She didn't regret what she had said at the meeting. On the contrary, she felt good about how she had said it. She had been angry, but she had remained calm. At least she had appeared calm.

*What now, Luvella?* If the other business people went ahead with the festival, they would fail—and fail miserably. None of them had ever done any successful marketing. But what about her business? She had had so many plans, little surprises, mark-downs on some of the things that had been here for a while.

She sighed a deep, long sigh and glanced out the front door window to see the hotel. *Maybe Anna will come soon, and I can tell her all about Luke.* There was no sign of Anna coming across the street, though. The thought never occurred to her that Anna might not come.

Luvella swung down the aisle, wider now with those benches removed, worked her way around behind the desk, and put her lunch in the bottom right drawer. She pulled out her ledger, her pen, and inkwell. After looking at the display cases, she left the cork in her inkwell for now and set her bookkeeping tools precisely on the far corner of the desk, ready for when her customers came in. *Want to leave plenty of room for people to browse.*

She propped her crutches behind the desk against the wall, and using the cases and tables as aids, hobbled down the aisle, back to the entrance door. She turned to stand there and examined the caboose. *What will people see when they first walk in here?* She opened the door, stepped out on the small stoop, tried to wipe her mind clear, then re-entered the caboose.

The first thing she noticed was the desk, even though it was in the back. It certainly was a showpiece after Reeder's refinishing. Then she scrutinized everything—the tied-back curtains, the windows, the glassed display case and the wooden tables and shelves. Reeder—she recognized his workmanship—had used the two benches from the caboose, refinished them, and had them as tabletops on the left side of the aisle. Jake and Bill must have done the sanding, because Reeder could never have gotten all this finishing done in just a few days. The tables had nothing on them right now, but Luvella would change that soon.

*I'll space out the displays so people can see that beautiful wood.* Her brothers had sanded and shellacked the benches so a deep reddish-brown finish matched the mahogany of the desk, creating a warm ambiance. They glistened now in the sunlight peeking through the windows.

Luvella paced the width and length of the car. She used the last page of her ledger and, uncorking the inkwell and dipping her pen into it, wrote across the top: Luvella's Knit and Knacks. She had been thinking of a name for her new place of business, but still wasn't sure. *That will do for now*. Then, she wrote: *Approx. ten feet wide X approx. twenty-four feet long.* Eventually, she would describe the furnishings and furniture, giving each a value. She had read this was important to establish her "capital." She already had complete records on her inventory for sale, her cost, and her selling prices.

Her right leg ached from the standing and hopping on it. She sat on the chair behind her desk and looked at the two sides of the aisle. Reeder had left a small walking space behind the glassed case and table, on the right as you entered the caboose. And, the desk, also on the right, already had space behind it, which is where she was sitting.

"That means," Luvella thought out loud, "that those benches will have to remain tight up against the wall so there will be enough walking room in the aisle."

She studied that left side, where the benches were. "I need something at this end, to add a special touch and to fill in the space but not take up too much."

By the time she had eaten her lunch and thought and thought, Luvella decided to ask Steckie for some of those barrels that his nails came in. She could cover them, padding the tops for seats, and using part of other barrels to form a small curved back. The barrels were the perfect size to use for chairs sitting at a small tea table. If Reeder could build a corner cupboard where the back wall and the side wall met, a small round tea table and those little chairs, in front of the cupboard area, would make a perfect eye catcher for people entering the store.

She went through her Sears Roebuck catalog to select fabric and colors and cotton batting. Now she was excited; her spirits were lifted; she had a new mission.

*I could go see Steckie right now, but I don't want to miss any customers.* She looked out her windows. No one was coming toward her store. *It's odd that Anna hasn't come to see me yet. I hope she hasn't taken ill.*

She printed a small sign for her door. "I'll be back in ten minutes." Then she went as quickly as she could on her crutches to Steckie's hardware store.

"Luvella!" Steckie said when she came through the door, balancing and turning. He didn't sound really happy to see her, just surprised. The stress of the morning meeting came back in waves. She stood still a moment, wondering if she should leave.

*No! The meeting was this morning. It's over. This is now.*

"Steckie." She smiled to encourage herself as much

as Steckie. “You know those small barrels that you get your nails in? Don’t you just throw them out sometimes?”

“Ayup, I do.” He smiled back. “Do you need some?”

“Well, yes, as a matter of fact. I think they’d be perfect for some small chairs I could make for my caboose. Do you have, maybe, three that you don’t want?”

“I have two right now. They’ve been in the back room for a while, so they’ll be dusty. And I’ll get more nails this week, on the next train from Pittsburgh.” He disappeared into the back storeroom and then came back with the two barrels. “I can bring them to the caboose for you.”

“That’s good, Steckie. Daddy can help me bring them home tonight.” She looked at how Steckie had filled in the corner space where her store business had been. “Where is everyone today? I haven’t had one customer!”

Steckie was quiet. Luvella turned to look at him. When she saw his face, flushed, his mouth moving with no words able to come out, she knew.

“Steckie,” she said. “I’m the one who should be angry, shunning them.”

Steckie nodded. “I know, Luvella. But these are just plain folk. They believe everything they read in the news, or more like it, all the rumors they hear about Indians. They’re afraid! And on top of that, you’ve abandoned them—your partners in business, your friends.”

“It’s more like they’ve abandoned me,” Luvella retorted. “This festival, with the whole town working together, would be so good for us." She was shaking her head. "I can't imagine them letting that go."

"Well-ll," Steckie murmured. "Like I said, they're afraid of the Indians. We…um…they didn't see them like you did." He began rearranging some tools, then put them right back where they had been.

Luvella watched him. *He's not really on my side with this, my own brother-in-law.* She turned toward the door. "Thank you for the barrels, Steckie."

She saw Mr. Johannson rushing up the step to the porch and into the hardware store. He nodded at Luvella, intent on his purpose.

"Steckie, I just got a telegraph from Hughsville. That Mr. Bocke is quite well known there." He grinned with success. "Appears he plans to buy a big hotel there, too. Has the present owner all worried, just like Ben here. Bocke keeps pushing to buy soon, buy soon, and he's only offering about two-thirds of the value." Mr. Johannson held the telegraph in one hand and slapped it with the back of his other hand.

"Here's the clincher, Steckie. The sheriff there is a good friend of the hotel owner and is looking into Bocke's finances. He doesn't have any money in the Hughsville Bank, and so far, the sheriff can't find his money anywhere.

"The sheriff found his name mentioned in a couple other towns—Boswell and Johnstown. Bocke promises money to owners of hotels that are wobbly, money-wise. The thing is, once his name is on the deed, he gets the income from the hotels. So far, the sheriff couldn't find that he's broken any laws. But he said to be careful of Bocke's offers."

Steckie said, "I knew there was something shady

about him. He just acted too…too uppity."

Luvella looked at Mr. Johannson. "Do you think you ought to wire that sheriff right away and tell him Mr. Bocke is here in Muncy Valley, trying to badger poor Mr. Smythe? And trying to buy my caboose?"

"Ayup, I did that already, Luvella. And now, I better go tell Ben. I don't know if that's good news or bad news for Ben, though. But at least he won't give up the deed to his hotel to that fleecer."

Luvella thought a moment, frowning. "You know, I saw Mr. Bocke come out of the bank one day, a good week ago. Maybe you should talk to Mr. Harley."

"Ayup," said Mr. Johannson. Suddenly, he looked at Luvella and stammered for words. He had been so excited, Luvella figured, he'd forgotten the meeting and the whole group's censure of her.

"I was just leaving," Luvella murmured and went out the door.

Back at the caboose, Luvella was startled when she opened her door. There was Mrs. Maarten, standing in the aisle, holding her reticule in both hands. She shifted her weight nervously from one foot to the other, and her face was wrinkled with worry.

"Hello, Luvella. I saw your sign and decided to wait for you." She looked all around, her head turning in jittery jerks. "This is very nice in here." She accented the 'very.'

"Thank you, Mrs. Maarten." Luvella had never seen Mrs. Maarten so fidgety. "Do you have some goods for me?"

Mrs. Maarten shook her head. "Luvella…umm, Luvella…I think this morning… I don't know… Oh Luvella, we just can't not have the festival." She had raised her voice, just a little, but that was a lot for Mrs. Maarten. "I couldn't say nothin' at the meeting, especially with my Erik not there. I'm just a housewife who makes things for your store. Nobody would listen to me. But it isn't right. The festival is such a good plan for us, for Muncy Valley. I don't know what to do, but I'm here to help you. Can we knock some sense into those noggins?"

Luvella stared for just a moment, then pointed toward the desk with one crutch. "There are two chairs behind there," she said. "Let's the two of us sit down and see what we can do."

# Chapter Seventeen

"I don't have a fire in the stove, it's been so nice and warm." Luvella pointed to the center of the left wall of the caboose. "If I had it now, I could make us some coffee." She smiled.

"No need." Mrs. Maarten waved her hand in dismissal. "What we have to do is somehow get everybody together again. I mean, together in our minds to do things." She patted her hand on the desk to emphasize her idea.

"Time is ticking away, you know." Luvella pursed her lips and shook her head. "To make the bonanza work, we have to send our advertising to *Harper's* magazine right now so the big city people will see it and want to come here. This bonanza is still a new idea, even for the big cities, and city folk would love our beautiful mountain view."

Luvella frowned in concentration, tapping her good foot on a rung of the chair. "Those Indians I was with were so nice. They're good people, kind and gentle. If only Muncy Valley folk could see that, could see them."

Mrs. Maarten slapped the desk top again. "Well, then, let's have them meet each other!" She bobbed her head and turned to look at Luvella straight on.

The two women sat like that, looking at each other, thoughts and ideas darting around like flies before a heavy rain. Finally, Mrs. Maarten asked in an I-hope-you-don't-think-I'm-silly tone, "Is someone having a birthday soon? We could maybe have a big birthday party?"

They both laughed.

"We could have a Founder's Birthday Party, but I don't even know when Muncy Valley was founded," Luvella said. "And besides, the Muncees were here first."

They were quiet again, thinking.

"If we could only think of something that would interest the men," Mrs. Maarten said. "Like football. I know if someone mentions football, the men gather round and even quiet Mr. Smythe raises his voice." She sniffed and rolled her eyes.

Luvella nodded, still pondering. Then, speaking as she thought, "I think…" She stood on her good leg and hugged Mrs. Maarten. Both blushed. "Mrs. Maarten, I think you've found our answer! My brothers play football with your husband and some of the other men sometimes. And Reeder and Bill just found out that Luke Raven, the Muncee who brought me home safely, is the famous linebacker at Carlisle."

Luvella took a step, planning to pace. The second she put her weight on her strapped ankle, she gasped in pain and sat back on the chair, raising her hand to Mrs. Maarten that she was fine. She needed to put her thoughts, swirling around in her brain, in some kind of order.

Finally, she said, "Mrs. Maarten, I think my brothers would go wild at a chance to play—and *win*—a game of football against the men who live in the tenant houses and their friends. They're a really rough bunch, Reeder told me, and usually win because they don't follow the rules. What if we had Luke and a couple of his Indian friends—from Carlisle—play on our team, on our Muncy Valley men's team?"

Mrs. Maarten gasped. "Erik loves the Carlisle team, and nearly had a heart attack from excitement when they beat Harvard recently. Oh, Luvella! You are so wicked!"

"I know." Luvella giggled. "Reeder says that all the time."

Mrs. Maarten puckered her mouth to one side. "I know Erik would do anything if he could play aside a Carlisle player. I've heard him rave about how good they are. And if we can have sort of an official game, all us women will be involved, too. Let's see, when could we have the game? How about the second Saturday from now?"

"Well," Luvella lied, "I know Luke had to go out of town for a while. He would be the one to get the other Carlisle players."

Luvella tore a sheet of paper from a pad under the desk, uncorked her inkwell, and dipped her pen. "Now! If the men want to have this football game, the Carlisle players would have a long trip. That means they couldn't get here, play a game and get back to Carlisle in one day." She thought about her family's barn. It would be insulting to have the Carlisle players all sleep in their barn. But if they slept in the house, would her brothers be willing to spend the night in the barn?

Mrs. Maarten was still pink from Luvella's hug, or maybe with excitement. She drummed her fingers on the desktop and stared, unseeing, out the back window. "Hmmm."

Luvella spoke as the thoughts entered her head. "I'll ask my brothers to go to the Muncees in Forksville, talk to Luke about getting some of Carlisle's players." She thought some more, long and hard. She shifted on her chair. "But the football game and Carlisle players aren't enough. We really need some basket makers to come to our game and bring their handiwork. And that's exactly what our friends don't want."

Mrs. Maarten glanced at Luvella, her face a complete blank.

Luvella was quiet, dismay all over her face. "Besides, the Muncees can't get here and go back in one day either, not if they travel in wagons." She pushed the hair back from her forehead with one hand.

"Oh Glory! They'll all have to stay overnight—the football players and the Muncee people. And I'm sure they can't afford Mr. Smythe's hotel, even if he'd let them in there."

Mrs. Maarten and Luvella frowned through more thinking, heavy thinking. Mrs. Maarten sighed.

"I'm sure I can talk Erik into having one couple stay with us, especially if he can also have a football player there. And if there's a single lady in their group, I know Mrs. Kiergen could put her up."

Luvella added, "I know Mama and Daddy would have Mr. and Mrs. Raven stay with them. I think my Uncle Isaac will still be in mourning." Then the idea hit Luvella like a thunderbolt. *Luke would be coming, too!*

She nodded, still thinking. "How will we let everyone know? We'll need more people to host the Muncees. I don't want to call a meeting. That is something they should ask me to do—if they ever do again."

Mrs. Maarten rested a hand on Luvella's arm. "Martha Johannson is my good friend. And so is Mrs. Kiergen. We will start with them and then spread the news. And Luvella…" She pointed her finger. "Let's not ask people; let's just go ahead and plan it. This is something we have to do."

The afternoon flew by. They decided to plan the football game as a rehearsal, so everyone could be prepared for the bonanza. They'd have the main road—in front of Mr. Smythe's hotel and most of the other businesses—be the football field, and the same set up they had discussed previously for the music and food. Women who wanted to sell their picnic meals would have to find their own baskets, or use cloths. Everything would be the same except for the merchants' sales and the baskets. "Maybe even out-of-town folk will come to watch the game." Luvella grinned. "This will be a big football game."

The sun was casting long shadows through the windows when they finished their plan. Each had tasks to do, right away. Luvella remembered to tell Mrs. Maarten about Mr. Johannson's discovery of Mr. Bocke's suspicious practices in other cities.

"I think none of us will be surprised about that" Mrs. Maarten raised her eyebrows and nodded. She added, "Mr. Smythe, I think, will be even more interested now in pursuing our football party plan. He needs to be interested!"

"I hope so. I hope so," Luvella said. "Have you noticed that not one customer has come in here today, Mrs. Maarten? Anna hasn't even come over!"

"They'll come round, Luvella. Just wait and see." She left her chair and walked around the desk and down the aisle. "Hasn't anyone bought my new scented soaps?"

"Not yet," Luvella answered. "But I was thinking… As I mentioned this morning, I'd like to get some really small baskets and put a cake of your scented soap in each little basket. Sell them as one package. I'll bet big city folk will love that, don't you think?"

"What a lovely idea!" Mrs. Maarten pretended she was an elegant city woman, picking up first this item and then another. "Oh my! These are all so chahming, I can't decide which to buy. I think I'll just buy *all* of them!"

They laughed together.

"Luvella, run over to see Anna right now. I'll stay here in case anyone happens to come in. Don't let the whole day go by without you seeing your best friend. And while you're over there"—she pointed her finger at Luvella again—"tell Mr. Smythe about our plan and tell him how many of us are for it."

Luvella looked blank. "How many of us are for it, Mrs. Maarten?"

"Why, all of us, Luvella. All of us. You tell him."

Luvella giggled almost all the way over to the hotel.

Once she opened the door to the hotel lobby, the sense of doom hit her like fog in a dip of the road. Anna was walking from the desk into the lobby, but when Mr. Smythe saw Luvella, he called Anna back. "Go to the office, please, and clean off the desk for me." Anna looked at Luvella as she backed away, her face sorrowful, her eyes wet and ringed in red. She didn't speak.

Luvella hesitated. Then, realizing Mr. Smythe must have heard about Mr. Bocke, she went to the desk. "Mr. Smythe! Just the person I wanted to see." She smiled with bravado and leaned on the desk to rest her arms from the crutches. "Has anyone come to you yet about our big football game celebration?" She ignored his frown.

"What football game? What celebration?" he echoed. "Nobody has said a word to me about it."

Luvella decided to forget about confronting Mr. Smythe with his dilemma of not having a buyer for his hotel. His mood was bad enough already.

"That's the point, Mr. Smythe. People are saying we already had made plans for a bonanza, so why don't we go ahead and have a football game instead? I heard they're going to see if some Carlisle boys will play on our team—against the tenant houses team. There, in front of your hotel, just like the bonanza. That is, if it's all right with you."

He looked up from his paper work. *Was that a glint of hope in his eyes?*

"You mean, I'd have food here for everybody?" he asked.

"Yes, sir. And there'll be music and dancing and a picnic after the game, just like we planned for the bonanza."

He came out from behind the desk. "Here, Luvella, you should sit down." He motioned toward one of the lobby chairs. "Get your weight off that broken ankle.

"So, when is this here celebration going to be?"

Anna peeked out from the office door and saw her father in conversation with Luvella. She smiled and came forward. "I've cleaned the desk top, Daddy." She sat on the arm of Luvella's chair.

Luvella patted Anna's hand. She was trying to figure out how to mention the Indians coming to the celebration. She said to Mr. Smythe, "A week from this coming Saturday. Everything else is the same as we talked about." She paused and moved her splinted ankle to a more comfortable spot.

"Except for a couple things," she added, adjusting her skirt. "I guess some people are concerned about not having the bonanza, about how that will hurt our town, and they're going to invite some Carlisle Indians to play on our team. The men are all excited about that, and that game alone will bring other townspeople in. People have decided to invite some other Muncees to join the celebration afterward, because they know we're going to win the game."

Mr. Smythe's smile faded. Luvella continued before he said anything. "Our neighbors here think we could meet them and see what they're like. They could also bring some baskets for us to inspect."

Mr. Smythe took a breath to speak, but Luvella kept on talking. "The only problem with the Muncees coming is that they would have to stay overnight. I don't think they could afford the hotel, so some of our people are offering their homes for the night."

Mr. Smythe paced over to the lobby desk, stopped, turned around, and came back to face Luvella. "Who are our neighbors, Luvella? What people have said they'll do this?" Suspicion mapped his face.

Luvella swallowed and hoped he didn't see it. "I'm not sure of all of them. But I know that Mr. and Mrs. Maarten, and Mrs. Kiergen, and Mr. and Mrs. Johannson are interested." She realized that Mrs.

Maarten was still in her caboose and wouldn't have gotten to Mrs. Johannson yet. *Oh, I've never gotten away with lying in my whole life. Why did I think I would now?*

She tried to stand. Anna helped her up. "Mr. Smythe, can they count on you to provide the food for this party? And can Anna come over to see some changes I've made in my caboose?" With Anna out of the hotel, she knew he wouldn't be able to run over to the depot to ask Mr. Johannson about the Indians staying at his house.

Anna must have detected Luvella's lie and jumped up from the arm of the chair. "Oh, thank you, Daddy. I won't be long." She made a show of helping Luvella hobble out of the lobby and down the stairs from the porch.

Back in the caboose, Luvella told Mrs. Maarten that Mr. Smythe was still reeling from what she had told him. "I think you'd better get to Mrs. Johannson right away. The sooner we get people together on this, the better," Luvella said.

Anna, looking from one to the other, said, "Luvella, I knew you were bluffing!" They all giggled. "But when I get back to the hotel, I'll ask Daddy lots of questions that will eventually bring him around." She opened her eyes wide, the epitome of innocence, and said in a falsetto voice, "What did Mr. Johannson say about Mr. Bocke? Ohh, hmmm. And does that mean that Mr. Bocke will not be able to pay us for the hotel? Ohh, hmmm. So, unless we have this football game in Muncy Valley—the bonanza would be even better—we may have to sell the hotel and move somewhere?" She covered her giggle with her hand. "That's how I always get him to agree with me."

Mrs. Maarten patted Luvella's hand. "I must go forward into battle," she said, "but softly, very softly." She grinned and waved goodbye.

Anna swung around to face Luvella. "Now! Tell me all about your Luke." They burst into laughter and settled onto the chairs behind the desk.

## Chapter Eighteen

Reeder and Bill stared at Luvella. Jake and Daddy walked into the kitchen from the porch and stopped.

"A game?" Reeder asked. "My little sister is planning a football game?" Mama had stopped stirring the stewed rhubarb and faced them all, her hand still holding the spoon over the kettle.

Luvella continued to set the table. "Mrs. Maarten came into my store today, and she was the only person to come all day, by the bye. Well, I dragged Anna over later, but I had no customers all day long." She shook her head, still unbelieving. "Anyway, Mrs. Maarten thought about a football game because her husband had been all excited about Luke Raven having been in town. You know, with him playing for the Carlisle team and all. And she felt awful about not having the bonanza."

As the men washed up for dinner, Luvella told them all that she and Mrs. Maarten had decided. She told them about her talk with Mr. Smythe, and that Anna was going to further convince her father to cooperate. She didn't share that part of her conversation with Anna, though; she didn't think Daddy needed to know the wiles and beguilement of daughters.

Reeder's black eyes glittered over a wide grin. "What d'ya think, Bill? Jake?" He dried his face and hands on the kitchen towel. "I bet Luke would love the chance to get back at those tenant guys. I know I would." The masculine rumble of get-even chuckles filled the kitchen.

Without waiting for an answer, Reeder said, "Luke told us he'd come for a game some time. This seems like a good time, except that Luke is on his…uh, out of town."

Jake cleared his throat. "Why do you want it so soon, Luvella?"

"Well, Mrs. Maarten and I think the Basket Bonanza is so necessary for Muncy Valley." She noticed Daddy nodding. "So if we have the football game soon and people here get to like the Indians—because we think we should have more than just Luke and other players from Carlisle, some of the basket makers, too—we'll still have time to plan and have the bonanza." She swallowed some milk from her glass.

"Of course, some of us will have to open our homes to the football players and to the visiting Muncees, too. Mrs. Maarten and Mrs. Kiergen already offered. And I think the Johannsons will, too."

Both Mama and Daddy stopped eating and stared at Luvella. Mama recovered first. "We could certainly have the Ravens all stay here."

Daddy set his fork on his plate. "You know, Margaret, I think that's a good idea."

Jake closed his eyes, set his mouth in a tight line, and furrowed his eyebrows. After a few moments like that, he sat at the table to eat. "Here's what I think." He pointed his fork at Reeder. "I think Bill and I could take on your load at the sawmill tomorrow, if that's all right with you, Daddy."

Daddy nodded agreement.

"And you, Reeder, could ride hard up to Forksville.

Maybe Luke finished his…trip out of town already. Maybe not. But you can talk to his folks and tell them about the game. Maybe there's someone else there who can go to Carlisle and get a couple other players.

"Wasn't Luke saying that Pop Warner had some 'blocking dummies' at Carlisle?"

"Ayup!" Reeder and Bill said together. Reeder added, "Maybe they could bring one here for us to practice with before the game."

"What's a blocking dummy?" Luvella asked.

Bill, sitting at the table, held up one hand to about two feet above his head. "It's a big bag, filled with cracked corn, I think. Long metal prongs on the bottom, pushed into the ground, lets it stand up in the field. The team tackles it in practice, just as if it was another player."

Mama spoke, getting everyone's attention as she passed a platter of meat to Jake. "Maybe we could make one for ourselves."

"Well-ll"—Bill's mouth scrunched up, making one eye almost wink—"it would take an awful lot of cracked corn away from our chickens."

"Hmm," Daddy said. "Would sawdust work?"

Jake dropped his fork onto his plate, the clatter bringing all eyes to him. "You are really something. Sawdust would be perfect." He took his serving of fried chicken and passed the platter to Bill. "But we'd need something really strong to put it in, so we don't have sawdust all over."

For a few moments, the only sounds in the large room were bowls being passed, spoons serving, knives cutting. Finally Reeder spoke. "Where's that old piece of canvas we used to cover the hay? Would that be big enough?"

Luvella leaned back in her chair and released a long, quiet sigh. Mrs. Maarten was absolutely right. The excitement of having a football game with Carlisle players on our team was very contagious. She couldn't wait to hear tomorrow how Mrs. Maarten had made out with her husband and her friends.

The Anderssons started their day early the next morning, just as the sun was barely ground level with the forest. Reeder was packed with Mama's food and Daddy's gun and left immediately after he ate eggs, bacon, home fries, and thick slabs of bread washed down with cold milk from the spring house. He gulped down a mug of hot coffee just before he mounted Daisy. "I'll see you just about twilight or a little after," he called back and departed in a brisk canter.

Luvella waved goodbye. "Watch out for the rattlers!" she said, her hands framing her mouth to direct her voice to him.

She could feel the eagerness, the intensity in her whole family. Even Mama said she'd start sewing the canvas today for the blocking tackle. So, it was with an early start Luvella rode the wagon with Daddy to the caboose. Her father talked to the horses, calming them. They were prancing down the mountain road, seemingly assuming their own version of football fever.

Entering the caboose, Luvella inhaled the piquant fragrance of Mrs. Maarten's lavender soaps and smiled, knowing her customers would have the same pleasure. She was barely finished putting her reticule behind the desk when Anna stomped up the steps and burst through the door.

"Luvella! I've been watching for you for hours, I

declare." Anna's face was pure cream, as usual, but there were tinges of pink on each cheekbone. "It took me most of last evening, but now Daddy's all interested in this football game. I think he'd really like to play on the team, but he knows it's best for him—and the hotel—if he stays to fix the food and keep the hotel ready for guests." She raised her shoulders and let out a huge sigh. "Have you heard from anyone else yet?"

"Anna! You realize how early it is, don't you? No one's out and about yet. But…"

Luvella began to tell Anna about her own family being so excited when the door opened again. Mrs. Maarten, a grin the size of a slice of cantaloupe on her face, sidled in. She waved her gloved hand and bent over at the waist, laughing hard. Luvella and Anna started laughing, too, just to see a very different, but delightful, Mrs. Maarten.

"Luvella, you too, Anna," she was finally able to say. "Erik is beside himself, thinking about playing football alongside Carlisle stars. One minute, he worries about having Indians all around us and the next minute he's bragging about having them here."

Anna nodded, her blonde curls bobbing. "Yes, Daddy's like that, too. But," she added, "can you imagine how hard it is for lots of people? Remember, we still hear stories about the tomahawk raids out west just about twenty years ago, and that's all some people know about Indians."

"I know, Anna," Luvella agreed, crimping her lips to a straight line. "But so much has changed in the last twenty years." She reached for paper, pen, and her inkwell. "Mrs. Maarten, your football game idea is the most brilliant one I've ever heard. How did Mrs.

Johannson and Mrs. Kiergen feel about it all?"

Mrs. Maarten started to laugh again, more like giggling. "I'm sorry, girls, but everyone has acted so excited about this that it just tickles me to watch them. Even Lars Johannson jumped up—I'm telling you, he jumped—to write down what he wanted to say on the telegraph and who he'd send the message to." She wiped a tear from one eye with her glove, still chuckling.

"Shall we get everyone together for another quick meeting, Luvella?" she asked, all business now. "We already have an idea of what to do because of our plans for the Basket Bonanza."

Luvella clicked her fingernails on the desk in rapid succession, forefinger, middle finger, ring finger, pinkie, over and over, sounding like a horse galloping in the distance. "I think we should let everyone work this out for themselves. Let them come forward, for a change, with ideas and suggestions. I think you talking personally to everyone has made the difference, Mrs. Maarten.

"The men will surely plan that game and make all the necessary arrangements. I heard Reeder say they could play on our main road, in front of the hotel and stores, even though it isn't as large as a regular football field. It's the best place, actually, Reeder said. They have to set markers or goals or something," Luvella continued, "but we don't have to worry at all about that. Reeder and Bill and Jake are taking care of everything for the game itself."

Mrs. Maarten laid her hands, one each on Luvella's and Anna's arms, and giggled again. "You will never guess who offered to have an Indian couple stay at his house."

Luvella and Anna stared.

"Mr. Melk?" Anna asked.

Mrs. Maarten shook her head. "Well, yes, he and Hilda said yes, too, but Mr. Harley overheard me talking about it at the post office, and he said Mrs. Harley was interested in having a couple stay with them when he told her about the bonanza. So he said the Harley home is definitely open for Indian guests. Luvella, we have oodles of room for our Indian friends."

A pain shot up Luvella's leg, and she realized she'd been standing on it the last few minutes. She slid her chair out from under the desk and sat on it. "Mrs. Maarten, can you organize things just like you were planning to for the bonanza? Try to have Mr. Smythe help you." She lifted her leg to rest it on the wastebasket next to her stool. "How many rooms do we have for the people from Forksville?"

Mrs. Maarten beamed. "First of all, Luvella, it's time you called me by my name, Thirza, since we're in cahoots together." She widened her smile and continued. "Well, we have the Melks, the Harleys, the Johannsons, Mrs. Kiergen—she can only have a woman—ourselves, and your family, Luvella."

Luvella had kept count. "That's at least eleven guests…Thirza," she said with an embarrassed grin. "You know, several of the people are not Indians; they're white. I know Mrs. Raven is white, and one of the ladies who helped me with Aunt Hilda is white. There may be more than that."

Mrs. Maarten patted her hair into place unnecessarily. "Ummm, my Erik would really like to have two of the Carlisle boys stay with us. I've never seen him so elated. He feels it's an honor to have those football players coming here, whether they're Indian or not."

"And he's right about that." Luvella nodded her head for emphasis. "I don't know how many Carlisle players will be able to come, but if Luke comes, he'll stay with my family." Luvella felt the heat rise to her face as Mrs. Maarten—Thirza—stared at her, and Anna put her head down to hide her grin. She rushed her words. "His family will already be with us, so it makes good sense."

When Thirza left the caboose with a swish of her long dress and the rapid clacks of her high-laced shoes on the boardwalk, Anna pursed her lips and squinted at Luvella.

"So, Luke will stay at your house, huh?"

The girls chuckled together.

Luvella said, "He'd better!"

****

Two weeks later, as she prepared for bed, Luvella went to her bedroom window and studied the mountain, bending to peer upward and leaning from right to left to see both sides, even in the dark. "I am asking you all—my God, the powers of the East, the West, the North and the South, Mother Earth and Father Sky—please help us all do the right thing tomorrow," she whispered. She closed her eyes to envision the trees nodding, and on the ground, the purple and yellow chrysanthemums and anemones waving. "We know tomorrow's football game is a good thing, and we know the celebration afterward is even better. Good people being with good people. Together, we can become our goal."

Her brows knit together with her intensity. “I can feel your…your support, like my crutches.” She stood there, with eyes closed, brows still pinched, and moving her head back and forth. “Please be everybody’s crutches tomorrow.”

She turned toward her bed. “Oh!” She twisted to face the window again. “Um, could you please bring Luke tomorrow, too?”

## Chapter Nineteen

After breakfast, Luvella cleaned her room and gathered an extra pillow and blanket for herself. Mr. and Mrs. Raven would be sleeping in her bedroom; she would sleep on the davenport downstairs.

Reeder, who had started and ended each day with tackling the dummy with his football friends and practicing “plays,” was assigned to killing and plucking the chickens for the picnic. At noon, Daddy, Jake, and Bill left with the wagon to meet the Muncees at Daddy’s sawmill. The host townspeople decided to all meet there. They didn’t want any men who might be at the tavern making trouble. Also, at that time, each family could lead their guests to their homes. The plan was to have the guests “settle in,” and then everyone go to the main road for the football game and the picnic in front of the hotel.

When she could hear the sounds of the horses’ hooves on the road coming up the mountain, Luvella hustled out to the porch and waited. Soon she saw Mr. and Mrs. Raven, sitting together on the driver’s bench of their wagon, following Daddy in his wagon, with Jake and Bill in the back. Luvella tried to hide her disappointment; she noticed immediately that Luke was not with them.

But she hobbled to the wagon to greet the Ravens, hugging Mrs. Raven warmly. “I am so glad to see you,” she said. "And now you can meet my mother. You'll love her." She said "Pleased to see you again" to Mr. Raven and led Mrs. Raven inside.

"How is Hannah?" Luvella asked, fairly bouncing with excitement, even on her crutches.

"Hannah is a very happy mother these days," Mrs. Raven beamed. "Little Matthew is five days old. But what has happened to you, Luvella?"

"Oh! Didn't Luke tell you?"

"No, I haven't seen Luke since the day after you left us. Have you seen him?" Mrs. Raven's face was suddenly serious, a mother's concern written all over it. "Did something happen to him?"

Luvella told how Luke had rescued her and brought her safely home. So he had met her parents and some other people in town. "He must still be on his vision quest," she ended.

"Oh, Luvella, please don't mention that," Mrs. Raven whispered, looking around. "That would be so dangerous for Luke, and all of us, if people learned of it."

"I only say it here, Mrs. Raven, because Luke explained it to my family when he brought me home. None of us will ever say a word about it, I promise. Here we are, Mama, this is Mrs. Raven. Her mother-in-law was Uncle Isaac's sister."

Mama rushed, with her arms open, to Mrs. Raven. "Let's see, that makes us friends and relatives." They both laughed. "Call me Margaret."

"And I am Elizabeth."

Mama had already poured mugs of coffee, and the women sat at the table, prepared to chat and get acquainted. Mr. Raven and Daddy came in with satchels that carried the Ravens' change of clothing and some sample baskets. The satchels were made of loosely woven soft reeds, with a drawstring closing at the top, and were perfect as bags for carrying clothing or anything. She knew better than to interrupt the conversation of the adults, but eventually there was an opening.

"Mrs. Raven, I've been sneaking peeks at your baskets there." She nodded toward the stack of three baskets near the door. "They're even prettier than I remember them."

Mrs. Raven blushed and smiled. "We are taking special care to make beautiful baskets for your bonanza," she said.

Luvella thought about telling the Ravens right then that the bonanza may not even happen, but she made an instant decision to not say anything. *Let's see how our football party turns out today.*

Then she asked, "Mrs. Raven, those satchels for your clothes…do you make them, too?"

"Oh, my yes," she answered. "But they're just for when we want to carry a lot of things easily. We use them when we pick our corn and apples, too." She tucked a tendril of loose hair behind her ear. "They're just, oh, what's the word? Handy." She laughed.

"Well, if you think you have time to make some of them for my store, then figure out what you need to charge me for them. I think some of my customers, even just from Muncy Valley, would love them."

Mama stood and started for the stove. "I'm going to get these chickens ready for the men to grill. The salads are all made, and everything's packed. Luvella, you show Mrs. Raven where the privy is and the room they'll be staying in tonight.

"Elizabeth, if you'd like to just lie down for a little while and rest from your trip here, we have a little time. Maybe half an hour?"

Mama had the time just right. The clock was chiming as they left the house, and all climbed into Daddy's wagon. Jake had arranged bales of hay and covered them with blankets as "passenger" benches in the back of the wagon so everyone could sit comfortably. They arrived to park along the side of the hotel a few minutes early, which Daddy had planned. As he reined in the horses, he turned to Mr. Raven and said in a confidential tone, "Good. We're here before Lars. Wait'll you see him pull up in his Model T, John." Daddy, Jake, and Bill all laughed.

Luvella said, "Daddy, he might not drive that today. I don't think everyone will fit in it."

"Oh, he'll drive it, even if he has to put Martha on the roof." Even John and the women joined Daddy laughing.

As if on cue, the putt-putt and rumble sounds of the Model T reached them from down the road. The Ravens stood and stared. Mr. Johannson honked and honked. *Ah-ooga! Ah-ooga!* Other people who had gathered, including Mr. and Mrs. Smythe and Anna, all laughed and waved. It was the only car in town, so it provided everyone's entertainment whenever Mr. Johannson drove it. When he got close, they could see Mr. and Mrs. Greycloud in the back seat, Mrs. Greycloud's eyes wide with fear, Mr. Greycloud's mouth clamped in a thin line.

Daddy squeezed between Luvella and Mrs. Raven. "You two better go welcome the little lady and help her get her breath back."

Already, the hellos, the howdys, the how-do-you-dos echoed through the crowd, which was growing by the minute, and mingled with laughter. Luvella noted with hope and a little satisfaction that, so far, this was like any other picnic the town had had. Everybody was friendly, even warm.

Reeder disappeared when the Maartens and Melks brought their guests, the Carlisle players. The football "team" ran to the yard behind the hotel, where Luvella heard their grunts and calls and the thuds when they practiced tackling the dummy. She looked at the sawhorses and barrels and portable hitches Mr. Maarten and Mr. Melk and Mr. Johannson had placed alongside the road to mark the sidelines of the football "field." At either end was a rope across the width of road, tied from one porch support to another. Reeder had told her those were the "end zones."

Anna came next to her. "Luvella, everyone is so excited and downright happy." She giggled. "Reeder came to Daddy and asked him to play on the team. They were one man short. And my Daddy is *sooooo* thrilled.

"Which means I suddenly have a lot of work to do. What are those barriers everywhere, Luvella?"

Luvella raised her brows in a scholarly fashion, and said, "Those, my dear, are the sidelines"—she pointed to the sawhorses and barrels—"and end zones." She pointed to the ropes at either end of the road-football field.

Anna curled her nose. "Oh yes!"

Some of the men had started the fire in the large fire pit at dawn, and the coals were ready for roasting the chickens, which they said they'd start at half-time. The women were spreading tablecloths and holding them down with dishes of baked beans, applesauce, and homemade pies on the long tables Daddy had sent over from his lumber mill. They put the cold salads in Mr. Smythe's large spring house. Mr. Johannson and Mr. Pearson were setting up their music and fiddles on the hotel's porch when Luvella, busy at the table with Mama, noticed a sudden quiet settle on the crowd.

Her stomach dropped, as if she had just bounced over a hill in the wagon. *Oh please. Don't let this be trouble.* She looked up and followed people's gazes to see what had caused the silence.

Pulling his surrey into the far end of the side of the hotel was Mr. Harley, the banker. Sitting next to him in the surrey was a woman. With them were Mr. and Mrs. White, both Indians from Forksville. Even though Mr. Harley'd lived in town for six months, no one had ever met his wife and now, Luvella was thinking, we all know why.

She was an Indian. She was remarkably beautiful, Luvella thought. *Like Hannah.* She could see the Harleys' hesitation, the awkwardness they felt as everyone stared at them. They were still in the surrey. Mr. Harley was spending a long time checking the brake and arranging the reins.

Luvella looked at Mr. Smythe, standing with Anna in front of the porch and staring, too. She rushed over to him. "Mr. Smythe, please come with me to welcome Mr. and Mrs. Harley and their guests?"

He looked at her as if she were crazy. Then Anna grabbed his arm. "Daddy, what a magnificent idea!" She actually pulled him along with her toward the surrey. "Mr. Harley is definitely a friend you want to cultivate." She winked at Luvella.

Luvella walked on his opposite side, but just a little behind him, in case he needed a little push.

That small act of welcome seemed to turn the tide of the whole picnic. It was like the sun bursting over the mountain, warming and energizing everyone. Mama followed them to the surrey, and Daddy came from the fire pit. As Mr. and Mrs. Harley and the Whites joined the crowd around the tables, Mr. Harley introduced his wife, Helen, who smiled to expose perfect, even, white teeth and charming dimples. Her blue eyes made a striking contrast to her swarthy complexion and black hair. The bulk of the front of her dress hinted at a new little Harley soon to join them. And Mrs. Harley then introduced the Whites.

At the tables, people were talking to whoever was at their side, nodding and smiling. The baskets were brought to the center table and examined by all the Muncy Valley women, *ohhing* and *ahhing* their approval. As Luvella suspected, they all agreed that the satchels would be a welcome addition to the different types of baskets. The women turned to their husbands and pointed out the beauty of the baskets, their strength, and—with straight faces—how brilliant their husbands were to decide to sell them at the bonanza.

Unfamiliar people and wagons arrived and hitched in spaces left between those wagons already tied up.

Mr. Johannson whispered to Luvella, "I telegraphed Dushore and Eagles Mere to invite people for the game." He blushed slightly and grinned. "I just happened to mention that some of the Carlisle team would be playing for Muncy Valley."

"Mr. Johannson!" Luvella laughed. "You are truly clever."

Loud singing and shouts brought their attention to a wagon full of men, racing into the center of the Valley from the tenant houses and Sonestown. When the driver braked, the men jumped down with brazen bravado. "Where's that li'l Injun team we're going to thrash today?" one man yelled as he swaggered toward the hotel.

Mr. Johannson leaned down to whisper again. "I'll take care of them, Luvella. You run and get Reeder. I think our game is about to begin."

## Chapter Twenty

Luvella sat at the picnic table with Mama, the Ravens, Mrs. Kiergen and her guest, and Mrs. Melk. Mr. Johannson walked over, introduced himself, and asked Mr. Raven to help him talk to the referee from Dushore.

"We've only got one referee, John," he said. "I hope he'll go ahead with the game." Mr. Johannson took off his hat, scratched his head, and put it back on. "With your son, Luke, being a famous football player—and I heard you know a lot about the game from him—maybe you could help referee. I also think it would be good for someone who isn't just for the other side, ya know what I mean? Whadda ya think?"

Mr. Raven, who had been shifting uneasily on the bench among all the women, stood up quickly. "We can ask him and see," he said, as they walked away to meet the man wearing black trousers, a white jacket, and a white straw boater hat. Luvella heard Mr. Raven add, "Whoever designed the center of this town must have had a football game in mind. This road is perfect, except for the wagon ruts here and there."

Luvella turned to Mrs. Raven. "This is the first football game I've ever watched. I'm not only excited, I'm nervous." She giggled. "I hope nobody gets hurt."

"Don't worry, Luvella." Mrs. Raven patted her hand. "I certainly know James and Matthew, from

Carlisle, will be in top form. Did you know that the Carlisle football team is the best? I'm sorry Luke isn't here. But I left a note for him, just in case he got home before we return."

Mama leaned toward Mrs. Raven. "Reeder and his friends have been pounding their bodies against that tackle dummy every day. They must be covered with bruises already." She shook her head and rolled her eyes upward.

A loud roar and men's whistles filled the air from the other end of the "field" as the Tenant Team, all wearing red shirts, sprinted out in a tight group. Then, from behind the hotel, whoops and shouts, in a sort of chilling rhythmic sing-song, pierced the air.

"Oh yes." Mrs. Raven chuckled. "That's part of Carlisle's program. They always enter the field with war chants—it really intimidates the opposite team."

Reeder led his team. They bent their bodies, pounding the ground, and chanted a strange song. Wearing blue shirts, they danced out to the center, and both teams lined up to face each other.

The official referee, in his comely jacket and boater, had a brief discussion with Mr. Raven and then walked over to Parson Schenkel, who stood at the fifty-yard line. Both men nodded, and the official returned to the center of the field. Shouting to be heard, he announced, "La-deez and Gentle-men! We'll all sing *The Star Spangled Banner,* and after that Parson Schenkel will open today's game with the coin toss."

The blend of male and female voices rising in unison to the highs and lows of *The Star Spangled Banner* raised goose bumps on Luvella's arms and, as always, brought tears of pride and respect to her eyes.

People settled on benches and blankets set out on the ground. The referee said something to the center of the Tenant Team. Mrs. Raven explained, "He's asking the visiting team to call the toss of the coin, heads or tails. If the guest team wins the toss, they get the ball kicked to them first. Otherwise our team does."

The teams drew back from the fifty-yard line, facing each other in opposing lines. Muncy's team won the toss, so the Tenants kicked off. The ball sailed end-over-end. James, one of the Carlisle players, anticipated the light kick and began to run forward. Failing to field it cleanly, he scooped it up, clutching it to his chest, and ran, but was stopped as the Tenants' coverage tackled him to the ground. He stood and held the ball up high. The Muncy Valley crowd cheered.

Mrs. Raven said, "Good. Our James can really run, so keep an eye on him."

Luvella watched, frowning her puzzlement, as both teams seemed to mill around the field, but then got in a squatting formation, two lines facing each other. She noticed James, Muncy's center, had the ball and snapped it to Matthew, his Carlisle teammate. Matthew turned left, trying to flank the opposing defenders. He headed toward the end zone with his right arm bent in a curve. The Tenants' defense ran to tackle Matthew. Mrs. Raven said, "Matthew's bluffing. Reeder has the ball!"

Almost simultaneously, the Tenants realized their folly and ran for Reeder. A particularly large man tackled Reeder near the sidelines, and as he fell to the ground, Reeder fumbled the ball on the Tenants' twenty-yard line. The opposition was quick to recover. The referee yelled, "Red ball!"

Roars rose on the summer air from both sides of the road, the Tenants' supporters cheering and Muncy's friends yelling.

The head referee gave the ball to the Tenants. After the snap of the ball, Mr. Melk tackled one of the men blocking for the runner, and Matthew flew through the air to grab the ball carrier around the knees. Luvella saw other players from both teams join the pile of bodies on the ground, arms and legs askew. They were almost in front of her table, clearly in her line of vision, and she marveled at how they unraveled from each other.

"Oh dear," Mrs. Raven murmured. Luvella noticed her brows were pinched with worry.

"I think, Mrs. Raven, that Luke has taught you well about football." She laughed, and Mrs. Raven's smile smoothed her forehead.

At the first time-out in the game, Luvella ran to where the Muncy team was gathered to see if they needed water or bandages. Reeder waved her off, as if she were an interloper. As she retreated, she heard James say, "You gotta place your feet just a little wider apart than your shoulder width." He was looking at the other team members—working men who rarely handled a football—circling around him. "When you tackle, get low, your feet set wide, and you smash up against his body, your back straight up"—James smacked one of his fists upward into his other hand—"and he's goners. It's all leverage. The smallest guy can take down the biggest one with proper leverage." Luvella cringed for that poor other guy.

Back at the table, Mama asked Luvella if the players were all right. "If they're not, it's their own fault." Luvella couldn't keep the bite out of her voice. "Reeder does not want me around there."

Mrs. Raven patted Luvella's hands. "They'll be fine, dear. Men love this game of warfare."

Through the game, Luvella watched the ball travel down the field, back and forth, under the hunched arm of a determined runner. Once, when the other side of the road erupted in cheers and Muncy's side yelled "Boo-oo! Boo-oo!" she saw the referees arguing.

Mrs. Raven said, "Oh, no! They can't do that!" Then she explained to Luvella that the Tenant player actually moved the ball back after they tackled Matthew so that our team had gone forward fewer than ten yards. "That means the Tenants get possession of the ball, and we're on our twenty-yard line. That referee isn't listening to John at all!"

Luvella had to wonder. *Is it because Mr. Raven is an Indian?* She feared it was and hoped again that it will be the only incident of that kind of behavior.

Although the teams lined up, ran a-scatter, and continually created a human stack of protruding arms and legs, the Tenants got the ball to their end zone. Finally, the teams ran off the field to their respective camps. Mrs. Raven stood and stretched. "This is half time, and they're ahead, six to nothing, but they're cheating. At least our team is playing a clean game. And now the men will have a few minutes to rest and plan their attack for the second half."

Luvella said, "I'll go see if Anna needs any help."

Inside the hotel lobby, several guests watched the game through the front windows, so she proceeded into the office. "Anna," she whispered. "Do you need anything? Something I can do?"

"Oh, Luvella. Glory, yes. Could you take these towels and place them on the dry sink in Room 102? I just signed in another couple. They're watching the game right now." She stuck out her lower lip and blew air upward, temporarily maneuvering the damp hair on her forehead. "I can take care of the rest. Thank you so much. And be careful on those stairs with your crutches!"

She turned back to her desk. Feeling a little rebuffed by Anna's too-busy-to-talk attitude, Luvella performed her task and peeked out the upstairs window to the side yard below. She saw the back of a familiar shape scoot from the side of the hotel and continue to the road. She ignored it, thinking instead, as she clumped down the stairs, of how both Reeder and Anna had brushed her off.

"Hmm. I guess nobody wants me around today," she whimpered, and wandered out to the front veranda. The women at her table, below, were talking together, all looking at Mrs. Raven, whose smile brightened her whole face. A clamor from the back yard of the hotel, where the Muncy team was, made Luvella look around for the cause.

Immediately, she saw Luke running from the road past the veranda to where the team was camped. His eyes met hers and he smiled. Her mouth, suddenly bone dry, stretched to a full grin, and her heart leaped. She almost ran down to him, crutches notwithstanding, but she realized he was continuing directly to the team.

From her higher veranda vantage point, she gazed around to see the tall man with carrot-red hair under a natty derby hat leave the Tenants' camp. "Now, what sort of business is our Mr. Bocke stirring up over there?" she mused, remembering the person sneaking from the hotel minutes ago.

When the teams lined up for the beginning of the second half, there was Luke, standing behind the rest of the Muncy team, poised like a mountain lion ready for the kill. James turned his head to the men directly behind him, but Luvella saw him glance at Luke and Luke nod ever so slightly.

Mama said, "Oh dear! They're up to something. I can feel it in the air. And I think the other team is, too."

"I know, Mama," Luvella whispered. "I just saw Mr. Bocke walk away from them, and I think he'd been behind the hotel, close to where our team was. Do you think he'd be low enough to spy on them?"

Although Mrs. Raven's wrinkled brow bespoke her concern, she said, "Don't worry. With three Carlisle boys and Reeder out there now, the other team doesn't stand a chance. And Luke is an excellent linebacker." She said that matter-of-factly, but not without some pride.

Suddenly the ball flew toward the other team.

Mrs. Raven gasped. "I don't think a pass like that is allowed. But the referee didn't whistle."

The one who caught it ran forward, supposedly planning to go through the middle of Muncy's coverage. Luvella watched Luke, dancing sideways a little, scanning the opposite team's players, and then cut downfield straight at them. Clumps of dirt kicked up as his feet dug into the road. He closed in on the other team and zigged to one side. He broke down, smashed into two Tenants and knocked them and the ball carrier to the dirt road.

"Ouch!" Luvella closed her eyes in empathetic

pain, and whispered to Mama, "I think that ball carrier was the man who kicked Luke that night outside the tavern. I'll bet Luke is enjoying this."

The Tenants' ball hadn't moved more than three yards, and Mrs. Raven was nodding in favor. "Both teams are really fired up. They will be very focused this half," she said.

## Chapter Twenty-One

The game seemed to move much more quickly this half because the plays were so intense. In the fourth quarter, Luke tackled the Tenants' quarterback, who flipped the ball to another Tenant. James leaped forward and snagged the pigskin. He passed it back to Reeder, who sprinted thirty-yards for a touchdown. Score: Seven to Six!

The crowd exploded. To whistles and hoorays, and boos from the other side, the two teams lined up. The kick-off bought a ten-yard penalty for Muncy Valley.

Mrs. Raven jumped up from her bench. "That is not fair!" she cried. "That referee is definitely out to get our team."

Fair or not, Reeder had to kick off from Muncy's twenty-five-yard line. As Luvella watched her brother position himself, she noticed Mr. Bocke moving briskly along the sidelines toward Muncy's end zone. Before she could process that strange action, roars and shouts brought her focus back to the game.

The Tenants' return man caught the football and took off for their end zone. Matthew brought him to the ground, but not before their returner lateraled the ball to another player, who then tossed it to a third Tenant. This time Reeder, James, and Matthew tackled the ball carrier, who flipped the ball in desperation over his shoulder.

Luke caught that careless toss, cradled it to his chest, and ran. He plowed through two of the Tenants' defensive players and was almost in for the score.

Suddenly, Mr. Bocke ran onto the field. Although he appeared bent on just crossing to the other side, he dodged back and forth to block Luke's progress. Luke zigged then tried to zag around the man. Mr. Bocke danced before him. Luke then barreled straight ahead, stiff-arming the red-haired man. Mr. Bocke lost his balance, but instead of falling, he performed an awkward chicken dance, with his arms flailing and his legs struggling for control.

At first, everyone guffawed. Then the referee's whistle announced the end of the game—but Luke had already touched the ball to the ground in their end zone.

The referee blew his whistle again and pointed his arm toward our end zone. "Munnn-cyyy Valley!"

Pandemonium exploded. Luvella stood, her fists pounding the table, and screamed, "Yaayyyy!" Even Mama clapped her hands and laughed, rocking back and forth. Apparently Luke had replaced Mr. Smythe, who was back at the hotel, on Muncy's team. But out on his veranda, Mr. Smythe unceremoniously put two fingers in his mouth and produced an ear-splitting whistle. He clasped his hands above his head in a victory sign to his team and returned into his hotel, smiling like the sun itself.

## Chapter Twenty-Two

Victory has a flavor all its own, robust and sweet. But the day's festive spirit had permeated the Valley even before the game. Everyone wore smiles.

All through the game, Mrs. Kiergen never left the side of Mrs. Carson, who had come from Forksville with the Ravens and would stay the night at Mrs. Kiergen's small second-story apartment. Every time Luvella looked at them, they were talking and giggling with each other, and once even clapping their hands together as they rocked with laughter.

Daddy, Reeder, Luke, the rest of our team, and Mr. Raven walked together over to the Tenants' team and shook hands all around. They had invited them and their families to bring dishes to pass and stay for the picnic after the game. Now, Luvella knew, they were extending an invitation again and reminding them that this is a family affair. Luvella watched as the Tenants shifted their weight from foot to foot and nodded. *They're embarrassed. They're probably decent men, if you take them individually.*

The food brought everyone to the tables. Luvella noticed with relief that the Indian guests, even the football players, sat with their hosts. Mrs. Raven faced Mrs. Harley, seated across the table, and asked what tribe she was from. Although she blushed, Mrs. Harley answered, "My mother is a Susquehannock, and my father is from Ireland."

Mrs. Greycloud said that there are many Susquehannocks still in the general area. "This was their country, too," she said. "The Muncees and the Susquehannocks—well, we're all part of the Delawares." The Indian discussion just flowed in and out of the whole conversation, like sugar dissolving in water, Luvella marveled.

She heard Mama praise Mrs. Raven's cornbread and Mrs. Greycloud's tomatoes. And Mrs. Raven wanted Mama's recipe for her rhubarb pie. The men gestured and recapitulated the plays of the football game, slapping James and Matthew and Luke on the back in obvious pride to be that intimate with Carlisle football stars.

As their excitement quieted, the men debated the merits, or lack thereof, of the Panama Canal. Luvella watched Bill listen to the discussion. She had overheard him telling Jake that he wanted to go down and work on the canal. She knew Mama wouldn't like that. So did Bill.

Mr. Raven asked, "Are you going to have hay rides and things like that at your bonanza? I'd be glad to drive my wagon for some of the hayrides." He thought a minute. "Big city folk would love to have an Indian drive them on a hayride." Laughter all around, guffaws from some of the men.

Luvella took note. The Muncy Valley people were actually proud of sitting at a table with Indians, like they were leaders of America, they were setting an example, they were the new pilgrims. And friendships had definitely been forged.

Daddy nodded to Mr. Raven. "Good idea, John.

One of my boys could drive a wagon, too."

Mrs. Maarten pulled Luvella aside and whispered, "Luvella, Sarah Kiergen and I have been talking to people today. Everyone is willing to have the Indians stay with them again and wants the bonanza to go on as planned. Maybe you should announce it today?"

"Oh no," Luvella whispered back, shaking her head. "The men are the ones who always speak up in our meetings, but they didn't say a word when I asked about bringing the Muncees here." Her eyes flashed anger. "If they want to continue planning the bonanza, with me leading, then they have to ask me."

Mrs. Maarten frowned, although nodding her head, went back to her table and sat next to her husband. But she did not sit quietly. "Erik could drive a hay wagon, too, right Erik?" She looked at him.

"Why, sure! I didn't even think of that." He blushed all the way into his thick blond hair.

Mrs. Maarten continued, as if she were on a mission. Which, in fact, she was. "Sarah Kiergen and I could have a taffy pull for the children. And what about a target shoot?"

"Why bother?" the new, very jovial, Mr. Smythe said. "Just give the blue ribbon to Luvella right now." Everybody laughed and looked at Luvella.

Reeder spoke from the fringes of the group, where the football players had gathered. "We could have a horse race, too." Mr. Melk liked that. "Ya. Ya. Gut!"

After each suggestion, the business people glanced at Luvella. She ignored them, although she was hoping with all her heart that the bonanza would go on.

After the women cleared the tables and packed the utensils and leftovers, which the men carried to the wagons, Luvella invited the women to come see her caboose. Mrs. Maarten made a show of saying, "I've seen it, as you know, and it's beautiful. I'll let the others see it, and then I'll be there again with some more things for you in a couple days." She gave Luvella a There-that'll-bring-'em-back look.

In the caboose, Luvella held up Mrs. Maarten's scented soaps and asked Mrs. Raven and Mrs. Greycloud if they could make really small baskets, just to hold a cake of soap. The Forksville women nodded exuberant yesses.

"Where *do* you get all these ideas, Luvella? You are so clever." Mrs. Kiergen spoke up from behind the others.

Luvella laughed. "From my *Harper's* magazine," she said. "It may not have baskets holding soaps in there, but something they had probably made me think of it. I'm not clever. I just like to read *Harper's*."

"But even this caboose idea, Luvella," Mrs. Kiergen insisted, looking all around. "You certainly know how to do business."

Luvella glanced back to see Mama looking at her and grinning when their eyes met. *Mama finally approves my caboose.*

The women filed out of the caboose, just as Reeder was sauntering across the road with some of his friends. Luvella followed the focus of their eyes, turned toward the privy behind the train depot, and saw Mr. Bocke there. She looked at Reeder, who gave her a wicked smirk.

"You just take your ladies back to the picnic, Sis. We're going to take care of our high-falutin' friend," he said.

"Reeder," Luvella whispered. "Don't you cause trouble and spoil this picnic."

"Never you mind, Sis. This will give everyone something else to celebrate." He and his friends guffawed. Luvella looked back, and Mr. Bocke had disappeared, probably inside the privy. She gave Reeder a frown and followed the women unsteadily toward the inn. Mr. Johannson and Mr. Pearson had just begun the music, and people were already dancing in front.

Moments later, a loud howl bellowed from behind the depot. The music stopped, the dancing stopped, and everybody turned toward the direction of the howl. There was Mr. Bocke, his trousers and drawers down around his knees, the Sears catalog placed modestly in front of his privates as he stood and looked all around him. The privy had been "tipped." Reeder and his friends had obviously pulled it over to expose the dandy at his most un-dandy moment. Nobody was in sight around the privy, although you could hear a group of males roaring with glee from the woods directly behind it, on the other side of the tracks.

The women turned away discreetly as the crowd on and around the dance area continued to snicker. Then the musicians tapped their feet for the downbeat and sang a few bars of *De Ol' Ark's a-Moverin'*.

*"See dat brother dressed so fine?*

*He ain't got religion on his mind.*

*Oh de ol' Ark's a mover-in', a mover-in', a mover-in'.*

*De ol' Ark's a mover-in' And I'm g'wine home."*

The people laughed and clapped their hands to the rhythm of the old folk song.

Nobody noticed Mr. Bocke after that.

Mr. Johannson announced a reel, and everyone got in position. Luvella sat and watched the dancers, which caused her the most pain of all since she broke her ankle. She loved to dance.

"How's your ankle behaving?" She turned to see Luke sitting down on the picnic bench beside her. He bent and gently picked up her foot, touching her loosely buttoned shoe around the ankle. "Still swollen, I see." He straightened up and looked at her.

She said, "Yes, but…" but her voice wouldn't cooperate; nothing came out. She cleared her throat, trying not to think about his hands touching her ankle, and spoke this time. "Yes, but it's a lot better. I've already started putting my weight on it in the caboose."

"That's good," he said. "It's going to take some time, but a little pressure for just a few minutes a day will strengthen it." He smiled, but his eyes, dark brown rings around his pupils, traveled her face. He stood. "I'll talk to you before we leave."

Luvella gaped at him. "Thank you, doctor," she managed. He grinned back at her.

Later, the sun was dropping to the treetops, and people were getting ready to leave. Mr. Johannson, still on the porch with his fiddle in its case now, called for everyone's attention. He cleared his throat and said, "Well, I think we've all had a good time today." Everybody cheered and clapped their hands. "We certainly had a good football game!" He shouted it and raised his fiddle in the air in triumph. Everyone clapped hands and hoorayed, and the men whistled. "Thank you, football teams, and especially the Carlisle players for helping us out." One gigantic roar filled the center of town as the horses snorted and swished their tails. Even the Tenants joined in. They would tell their families for many years to come about the game they played against the Carlisle team members.

Mr. Johannson's face turned serious as he continued. "I've been hearing everyone say they want to do this again." More cheering, "ayups," and people nodding. "Luvella, could we ask you to continue our plans for the Basket Bonanza?" Everyone looked at Luvella. "Please?" he added.

Luvella leaned on her crutches. *This is what I wanted! Why do I feel like telling him no, I'm finished fighting for every new idea?* She looked around her. People were smiling; they were happy; they were her friends! The game and picnic were a success beyond her hopes.

Daddy was looking at her and nodding. She pursed her lips, sucked in a deep sigh, and finally said, "We have lots to do and in a very short time. Let's get the business members together on the porch for just a few minutes."

## Chapter Twenty-Three

Daddy pushed the horses on the ride back. There was still some sunset afterglow to light their way, so he raced it home. Even with a lantern on the front of the wagon, it would be hard to see the wagon road on the mountain at night. On the way, he said, simply, "Luvella, good job."

Mrs. Raven added, "Luvella, I had no idea you were such a business person. Your caboose is…is wonderful! And you're still so young. Hannah would love to see it."

Mama said, "Luvella had some hard luck. We were all down with typhoid fever, and she had to take care of us. Will almost lost the sawmill, and she just took right over and started her little homemade crafts business. And it really grew and grew." Mama put her arm around Luvella's shoulders, giving her a little squeeze.

"Could Hannah come to the bonanza?" Luvella asked Mrs. Raven. "I really miss her. It's funny, my best friend's name is Anna, and I feel like Hannah's a best friend, too. Their names are almost the same."

Mrs. Raven nodded. "The Great Spirit has planned these special friends for you. You are blessed. We will see about Hannah coming to the bonanza."

"Well, here we are," Daddy announced, pulling into the drive. "Reeder and Bill, take the wagon. Jake, you and Luke help us unload here."

As Luvella lit a lantern and headed for the privy, she heard Mama ask Mrs. Raven, "So tell me about Aunt Hilda. Luvella was very touched by her, in fact, by all of you in Forksville…"

Sunday morning, Mama fixed a big breakfast, and Mrs. Raven and Luvella brought the brimming platters to the table. Steak from Mr. Pearson's General Store, home fried potatoes, fried eggs, the sweet and salty smells wafting everywhere, and, of course, hot coffee. "You have a long trip ahead of you," she said to the Ravens. "This will tide you over for most of it, and I'll give you food to eat for when you have a rest stop."

Saying goodbye was a mixture of sad and happy. Luke spent most of the time helping her brothers with chores or just talking to them about football and Carlisle and Pop Warner. "At least you'll be coming back soon, Elizabeth," Mama said. The whole family was at the Ravens' wagon.

As Mrs. Raven was placing her reticule in the back of the wagon, Luvella went to her and asked quietly. "Mrs. Raven, on your way home, could you ask Luke to come to the bonanza, too?"

Mrs. Raven looked at her, strangely at first. She hugged Luvella, then held her back away from her a little, peering into Luvella's eyes. "Oh, my dear!" She pulled Luvella into another hug. "Now I know what was bothering Luke just before he left on his quest. Of course, I'll ask him to come with us. But why don't you ask him right now?"

"Oh, no!" Luvella said. "Just tell him to come."

"I think he will need to hear that you invited him. Otherwise, he might not come."

Luvella swallowed the bile that had rushed to her

mouth and lowered her head. She looked up, then, and said, "All right, Mrs. Raven, tell him I'd really like it if he came to the bonanza." She turned just as he ran from the barn and jumped over the side and into the back of the wagon.

The Ravens left. Luke and Luvella looked only at each other, and his family continued to wave until they were out of sight. Mama and Luvella had to hurry to clean up from breakfast and be ready to leave for church. Luvella didn't even have time to talk to her mountain.

When Parson Schenkel stood for his sermon, he waited a moment and looked all around the small church. He read from the Gospel of Mark.

He closed his Bible and looked at the congregation again, nodding his head. "Yesterday, my dear people," he leaned on the lectern. "Yesterday I witnessed the kingdom of God." He stood straight again. "Yesterday, I witnessed Christianity in action. I saw it in front of your hotel, Ben; in front of your caboose, Luvella; in front of your depot, Lars; all over Muncy Valley." He swallowed hard, a deep red color flushing his face.

Silence penetrated the church. There wasn't a cough, a sniffle, or a shuffle of feet. Pastor Schenkel cleared his throat and said, at barely more than a whisper, "I am humbled. I am proud of you and truly humbled."

After the church service, people clustered in conversations, and from snatches she heard, Luvella knew they were all talking about yesterday's football game and the celebration afterward. They mentioned first one and then another of the Muncees, always a funny comment or story they had told. There were broad grins, deep chuckles, nodding heads, like her mountain on a sunshiny day.

Luvella walked over to Mrs. Maarten and said with a smile, "You must be exhausted today, Mrs…Thirza. You certainly did a lot of talking to certain people yesterday."

Mrs. Maarten opened her mouth, but the flattery seemed to make her speechless. Luvella laughed, then whispered, "That's all right. You saved our Basket Bonanza, Thirza. And I thank you very much."

Back home, she immediately began setting up the advertisement she wanted to send to the *New York Times*. The group had said last night to mention the fact that Indians would be here. Everyone felt that that would be an attraction more than a turn-aside. She wrote down the points she wanted to include in the advertisement: basket bonanza (beautiful Indian handmade baskets, all sizes and colors), each store would have items on sale plus regularly-priced items, the whole town a bonanza, hay rides, horse race, target shoot, and taffy pulls and pony rides for the children, a huge picnic for everyone, a hotel right in town, and some private homes to rent out rooms.

The next day, Luvella re-wrote the ad she had finally settled upon and stopped at the depot to ask Mr. Johannson to wire the *Times*, telling them that her ad is on its way for their August 1st and 8th issues. She was disappointed that they missed *Harper's* deadline, but at least the *New York Times* could run it. The other towns' papers would be no problem at all: Dushore's, Forksville's, Sayre's, Williamsport's.

As she approached the depot, Luvella knew she'd been smiling when she stopped—when she saw Mr.

Johannson's face, his lower lip pursed upward so that his whole face seemed to be curving downward.

"Uh, hullo, Luvella." His voice was lifeless, and he turned away from her to neaten a stack of wires that were already neat.

"Good morning, Mr. Johannson." Maybe she could cheer him up. She gave him the messages and addresses for her wires, and said, "Do you have your fiddle all warmed up for our bonanza?"

Mr. Johannson just shook his head back and forth, back and forth. "Oh, Luvella," he whispered.

*Oh my! He looks like he's almost going to cry.*

Still shaking his head, he said, "Luvella, that Mr. Bocke has been talking privately to the railroad about buying the caboose. I just found out now that they're considering letting him do it."

"But I have a lease!" Luvella said. "How can he do that? What will happen to my business?"

Mr. Johannson sighed. "He told the railroad that he'll just rent it to you until he decides to do something else. I guess he couldn't afford the hotel, Jude told me."

"Mr. Harley? What about him?" Luvella frowned.

Mr. Johannson tugged on his ear. "Jude said our Mr. Bocke gave the bank some warehouse receipts for a train carload of cotton bales. The receipts are collateral for a five hundred dollar loan. So now Mr. Bocke is bartering with the railroad. He told me he'd already had your lot surveyed. Did you see any surveyor around, Luvella?" He frowned his doubt.

"Goodness, no," Luvella answered. "I've been awful busy lately, but I'm sure I would have seen someone in my yard through one of my windows." She picked up the papers she'd written her ads on. "Mr.

Johannson, this is terrible news! I sure don't want to rent from him.

"I don't know now if I should even keep my business, or…or…" She stopped speaking, and her eyes darted around, not focusing on any one thing. "Unless Daddy and I together can outprice Mr. Bocke."

She looked up at the depot manager. "Mr. Johannson, could you let Daddy or me know if the railroad tells you anything that looks like they're going to accept his offer? I'd really like to know what the price he offered was, too. Or is it already too late for us to do anything?"

Mr. Johannson, still pulling his ear, said, "Well-ll, I heard the railroad is checking Mr. Bocke out pretty good. When the railroad comes back to him, I might be able to leave a wire from them right here on my counter when you come in. By mistake, of course. But I know the railroad, and they don't let go of their land easy. Let's just wait and see here."

On her way back to the caboose, Luvella felt her shoulders sag as she hung her head. The air felt like molasses; she could barely get through it. She concentrated on her shoes, first one toe, then the other, as they peered from under her skirt. She found herself counting her steps, as she had that day Mr. Johannson had led her from the depot.

*Thirteen steps—about thirty feet. Oh how nervous and excited I'd been that day! And all my plans and work since then!*

She pulled on the railing to plod up the steps and into her caboose, slowly closing the door behind her, leaning against it until she heard the click of the latch. Tears blurred her vision and streamed down her face.

Her knees felt as if they would buckle, like they did that night she arrived at Forksville.

*Forksville! Luke! How proud all of them are to be selling their baskets and to be part of our bonanza. And Mama, Daddy, my family—all their work and mine. We've painted the caboose, inside and out, scythed the grass on the property; I've even got flowers growing there now.*

Her legs weakened more, and her head felt like everything was draining from it. Clinging to the counters and tables for support, she found her desk and slumped into the chair there.

****

"Luvella! Luvella!" Are you all right?" Anna's voice. Someone shaking her shoulder, making her head slide back and forth on the desk. She opened her eyes. Her head was on the desk.

"Wha—?" she said, slowly pushing herself to a sitting position. "Oh…Anna…" Her head swam. And then she remembered.

"Oh, Anna!" she sobbed. "What am I going to do?"

Anna shushed her, patting her back, until Luvella became calm and told her about Mr. Bocke's threat.

"I thought it was strange that we hadn't seen him in our hotel," Anna said. "But Luvella, isn't it nice that you and I take turns having to fight the world?" She grinned and bent to face Luvella. "Now, let's find my old friend, Luvella—the one who owns her own business and almost runs our whole town." Luvella managed a wan smile. "My friend, Luvella, who promised me we would take care of Mr. Bocke."

Luvella sat up, remembering her own recent support of Anna. "Anna, thank you. You're right—and you're a very good friend."

"Now, Luvella, tonight you talk to your daddy about this. Don't wait. And you know that nobody in the Valley wants Mr. Bocke around. Nobody. Let's just keep our eyes open and continue with all our plans," Anna finished.

So it was that later that morning, Luvella forced herself to write the Pittsburgh Chamber of Commerce. "Now, where did I put that address?"

Poking through her ledger, she remembered. "Ah, right in my names and addresses section." She grinned to herself, beginning to feel better.

After the date and the address, she wrote:

*Dear Sirs:*

*The merchants in Muncy Valley, Penna. have had an organization for two years that sounds very much like your chamber of commerce. As such, we would like two things from you.*

*First, could you send me the requirements for establishing our group as a chamber of commerce; and second, would you please send me the information for our representative to attend your conference in October this year?*

She decided to not say thank you. "Just stick to business, Luvella." So she finished:

*Very truly yours,*

*L. Andersson*

"There!" She licked the stamp and pounded it soundly on the envelope.

Anna came over again later to eat lunch at the caboose—purposely avoiding bringing up Mr. Bocke—and they talked about a new sign. "I want a new name," Luvella said. "Something that mentions the caboose."

They giggled at some of their ideas: Kit and Caboose, Luvella's Caboose, (Anna said all the boys would love *that* one!), the Lost Caboose. Finally, they agreed on The Crafts Caboose. Luvella said she'd pick up some wood at Steckie's so Reeder could work on the sign right away.

Throughout the day, between the customers and visitors, Luvella worked on the first of her two barrel chairs, knowing that keeping busy was good medicine. The day went by so quickly, she barely had time to go to Steckie's to get the wood for her sign before Daddy was due to pick her up.

As she returned from Steckie's and re-entered her caboose—of course, she had left her door unlocked—she was surprised when a draft of air pulled her door closed behind her. Something was different! That innate sense of alarm raised gooseflesh on her, and she tiptoed to the back of the caboose to check her lock and door. The door was not only unlocked, but it was open. *That's why my door slammed. Someone had been in here and must have left by my back door!*

She quickly looked out through the door's window just in time to see that dreaded figure again, sneaking across the train tracks and into the woods behind her store. This time, Mr. Bocke was carrying his derby in his hands, but Luvella recognized his frame immediately.

*Why is he so sneaky? Because he knows no one likes him,* she answered her own question. *And because he's up to no good!*

When Daddy arrived, he inspected the property behind the caboose and into the woods a little. Luvella told him about Mr. Bocke pushing the railroad to buy her caboose and her conversation with Mr. Johannson.

"I'll talk to Lars tomorrow. I've done business with the railroad for years, so they know me and my business reputation, and I know the higher-ups there. Don't worry. This is definitely something I can handle." He winked at her.

In the weeks following, Mr. Raven and Mr. Greycloud took turns delivering baskets to the stores in Muncy Valley. The women rushed into the caboose after every delivery, even if they didn't have business with Luvella.

"Oh, Luvella. The colors. And I love the designs."

"Luvella, can you imagine the variety? How do they do that?"

"Oh my, Luvella. I hate to *sell* them. But where would I put them all?"

Luvella laughed with each one and then rushed back to her own work.

One of the Valley's men always met them at the crossroads, but there was no trouble coming from the tavern there. The tenants and their friends had been duly chastened at the football game. Still, that meeting arrangement wasn't changed; no one wanted problems for the Basket Bonanza.

Only Mr. Johannson and Luvella had seen Mr. Bocke in town since the football game. Mr. Smythe had a permanent smile on his face, it seemed. Luvella didn't know whether it was because Mr. Bocke was no longer threatening him or whether it was from all the room reservations coming through the mail for the bonanza. She suspected it was both.

Mr. Johannson came into the caboose one day, his eyes widening as he looked around at her expanding displays. "Just wanted you to know, Luvella, that Jude Harley is questioning those receipts Mr. Bocke gave him. Mr. Bocke keeps saying he's having problems selling the cotton and can't make any payments on his loan until he sells the cotton or owns the caboose and rents it out." He pointed his index finger.

"Meanwhile I've told the railroad that many people refuse to do business with him and that you are related to Willem Andersson, who will strongly recommend you." He cleared his throat. "I didn't say you were his daughter, of course." He blushed. "I told the railroad that my opinion was that they should wait for full payment from him before they sign any papers."

He put his hands in his pockets and nodded his head. "Luvella, all of us in the Valley are right behind you."

"Thank you, Mr. Johannson. Thank you. I'll tell Daddy what you said. And you'll tell us if we need to do anything?"

Nodding yes, he turned to go. "This is dandy in here. Are you sure it's the same caboose I rented to you?" He fumbled for the door handle and chortled on his way out.

Her days were so filled with business, working on her chairs, and checking on bonanza plans with everyone that Luvella never got to walk out the back door of the caboose to just look around, even though she no longer needed her crutches.

Until one day. She finished eating her lunch and decided to enjoy the sunshine. She stood on the back platform and, with her eyes closed, inhaled deeply. She smelled the scent of pine coming from the nearby woods, along the other side of the railroad tracks behind her. Flies and bees created a steady hum of music and somewhere, in the distance, a hound wailed, probably in harmony with a train whistle that Luvella could not yet hear.

She opened her eyes. *How peaceful it is here*. She turned in a complete circle, observing what was really around her. And there was her mountain.

For a moment, Luvella didn't breathe. The majesty of the mountain overwhelmed her. She studied it, ending at its very top. *You're touching Heaven. You are definitely a connection, between me and Heaven, between Uncle Isaac and Heaven, between Luke and Heaven.* She closed her eyes again. She hadn't thought about Luke for…almost an hour. She smiled. *But I can feel him now, here. Oh, how I wish...*

She sighed and went back into the caboose. She hoped again, for the thousandth time, that Luke would come to the bonanza.

## Chapter Twenty-Four

No sooner did Luvella get downstairs, than she had to run back upstairs to get something else from her room.

Mama said, "Luvella, I do declare. You make more noise now with all your running than you did when you clumped around on your crutches. Slow down before you're back on your crutches again."

Luvella smiled and kissed Mama on her forehead. "I think I have everything now, Mama. My room is all ready for the Ravens. Fresh water is in the pitcher for them, and a clean towel is folded on the table. I put some roses in our china vase there, too. Mrs. Raven loves roses, I heard her say."

Mama beamed. "After they get here and rest up a little, we'll be along. And if you need help in the caboose, I'll take care of Vanessa so Bessie can help you. Good luck, Luvella." She held up both hands with her fingers crossed. "And to all of us!"

Luvella twirled to show off her new lavender dress with the mutton sleeves. The skirt flared out in waves from her ankles.

"How do I look, Mama?"

Mama smiled. "You look beautiful, honey. Your waistline looks smaller than my leg." They laughed together.

Luvella rushed out to Daisy, all saddled by the

door. She wouldn't ride bareback today, even just to the caboose, because she didn't want Daisy's horse smell on her new dress. She threw the two satchels Mrs. Raven had made for her across the horse behind the saddle.

"'Bye, Mama!" she shouted from the hitch by the door, put her foot up into the stirrup, swung her other leg over Daisy. Adjusting her skirt properly around her to keep any wrinkles from forming, she *tsched* the horse to a brisk walk out the drive. Once she reached the road, she urged Daisy to a canter down the mountain and into the Valley. A small cloud of dust flew behind them as they reined up at the caboose. Luvella walked Daisy to the back, unsaddled and tethered her to the railing of the caboose's platform there.

She glanced around the Valley as she rushed to the front to unlock and enter the caboose. Men were setting up the picnic tables; the fire pit was prepared, and she could see the large spit holding the roasting pig; Mr. Melk ran from the picnic tables back to give the spit a turn; Mr. Smythe was sweeping the porch of his hotel, a white apron still tied around his middle. Luvella was sure he and Mrs. Smythe had had to cook breakfast for several guests. There would be many more coming today. Last she checked, he had only one room left.

*I wonder if Mr. Bocke will appear today. He hasn't bothered Mr. Johannson since that awful day when I caught him in my caboose. Or* almost *caught him. Daddy asked the sheriff from Dushore to be here today, just in case there were any problems.*

On her way up the steps, she noticed how spiffy her new sign, *The Crafts Caboose,* looked above the door. Reeder had painted the background bright white, painted a narrow black frame around it, and the name's letters were all barn red, matching the color of the caboose itself. She smiled now, remembering how hard she had hugged Reeder when she saw it for the first time. Reeder was so embarrassed, he actually blushed.

She entered the caboose, putting her key in the top desk drawer. The delicate lavender scent of Mrs. Maarten's soaps welcomed her again. "Mmmm, I hope all my customers today will enjoy that as much as I do," she said aloud, smiling her pleasure. "And then buy them."

Everything was perfectly displayed, sizes, colors, textures working together to create an ambiance of luxury, and her prices were set to make it all affordable. She had even set up her little tea table as her "Penny Table" for the day. Everything on it was priced at one, two or three pennies.

Reeder had whittled tiny canoes, bows and arrows, simple shapes easily made from sticks on the ground. Those were some of her penny items. Mr. Raven saw Reeder making them on one of his visits and, on his next delivery of baskets, brought small Indian dolls and tiny leather pouches, like the one Luke had worn around his neck. He offered them for Luvella's Penny Table, and she charged two cents for each of them. The arrangement was, with Reeder, for every two of his items she sold, Reeder would get one penny. Mr. Raven would get one cent for each of his items she sold.

She set her satchels on the floor behind the desk and went out the back door. She rubbed Daisy's nose and turned to face her mountain. The sun was near up to the timberline, and the sky was cloudless. Except for one. Luvella noticed it, wafting sublimely to the east.

*Junior! Oh Junior. Are you coming to our bonanza, too?* She smiled and inhaled, long and deeply.

She studied the mountain. A hush enveloped her. The sounds of the men working across the road, the rattle of wagons on their way to the sawmill crossroads, all were absorbed into the hush. *I always feel like I'm in church when I feel the strength of my mountain.* She remembered Uncle Isaac saying, "We are all connected. We are one with Mother Earth and Father Sky."

Her eyes feasted on the mountain. *Your trees all started from seeds. Look at them now. All sorts of animals—and men—are protected by them. Even the branches of your trees reach upward, as if they're praying. That's why I feel your strength and wisdom. You are reaching to Heaven, and you are much closer to Father Sky than I am.*

She stood there for several more minutes, breathing in the mountain's beauty, its comfort and its energy. She thought of Luke and knew he would understand what she was feeling and thinking now. *Oh, how I hope he comes to the bonanza today.* She looked again for that solitary cloud. It was not in sight. But she knew that it was up there, somewhere, and that Junior was, too.

Daisy nudged her elbow, startling her. "Yes, Daisy, I know," she said. "I have to get to work." She went back into the caboose. She emptied the satchels of some last-minute items, mostly from Reeder's whittling, and added them to her supply. Those that didn't fit on the display table, she hid under the table skirts until she would need them.

People were already strolling around the commercial area of the Valley, probably the hotel guests, Luvella decided. As they reached her caboose, she heard them through the open window expressing their pleasure at the idea of shopping in a caboose. Once inside, they remarked on the "lovely products" (one of them said) to choose from, and Luvella's day began.

The merchants had decided that every hour two boys would go from store to store to get a record of each person's sales and then show the report back to everyone. This way, everyone had a good idea of which products and presentations were more successful and still had time to perhaps alter their own. About two weeks ago, Luvella had met with all the merchants and gave them ideas of how to display their goods attractively, to encourage people to buy them.

Mama came into the caboose as Luvella rushed between the aisle to answer questions and the desk to take payments. Mama just waved and left. A few moments later, Bessie walked through the back door. She whispered to Luvella, "I'll take care of the desk and cash them out, like we used to do." Luvella smiled and mouthed "Thank you." She stayed at the front door to welcome people and to answer questions as they made their selections.

Although hours passed, it seemed like only a few minutes later when Hannah came in. Luvella rushed around some women in the store and threw her arms around Hannah's neck. "Ohhh, Hannah! How good it is to see you!" They laughed as some women pretended not to stare, although they all smiled.

"You remember Frank, don't you?" Hannah said. Luvella noticed Frank then, whom she hadn't really talked to when she was at Uncle Isaac's. She was surprised to notice that, although his skin was darkly sun-tanned, he was not an Indian.

"And this," Hannah interrupted her thoughts, "is Matthew."

Luvella reached for the little bundle, sound asleep, in Frank's arms. Little crescents of dark brown eyelashes framed his pink cheeks and a tuft of black hair pointed at his button nose. "Oh, Hannah, he's beautiful!" She bounced him gently, twisting back and forth. Then she turned and showed him to Bessie and the women customers in the store.

One of the women said, "I think his daddy deserves some credit, too." It was a special, shared moment, and Luvella hoped and prayed this was a preview of how the day would go.

Bessie held Hannah's hand in both her own. "I am so glad to finally meet you. Luvella raved about you so much, I wasn't sure you were real." Even the customers laughed and Bessie looked at Frank.

"Welcome to our little town," she said. "Are you all settled at my folks' home?"

Hannah smiled. "Frank and little Matthew and I will be sleeping in your brothers' room tonight, and Luke and your brothers are going to bunk in the barn."

They laughed and Frank added, "There are definitely advantages to being married." Hannah gave him a pretend-disgusted look, but her eyes brimmed with loving adoration.

"So Luke did come?" Luvella asked quietly.

Hannah grinned at her and at Bessie. "Yes, Luvella. Luke is here. Somewhere." She looked out the window with no confirmation. "Now! Show me your caboose!"

With so many customers coming and going, Luvella didn't keep track of the time. Bessie was still collecting payments and giving change while Luvella helped the buyers when one of the young boys came in. "Luvella!" His voice was loud and excited. "Target shoot!" He turned and ran across the street, as if the women in the store had terrified him.

Luvella looked back at Bessie. "You go ahead, Luvella." Bessie waved a hand at her. "I'll handle everything here. And if you ladies want to see our very own Annie Oakley, you can watch Luvella show her stuff at the target shoot."

As the women all turned as one to look at Luvella, she grinned and gracefully stepped down the stairs of the caboose's front platform. Then she ran across the road to where the target shoot was being held.

The hay wagons and pony were tethered at the hotel's hitches. A large crowd had gathered. The people who had signed up for the shooting competition stood at the picnic tables, forming a line. Luvella scooted into the last place, her usual position. She liked to see how the other shooters performed before she took her turn. The target bottles were lined up on the fence alongside and slightly behind the hotel.

"Save the little bottles for Luvella," someone shouted. She recognized Reeder's voice. All the men laughed and one of them retorted, "Ayup. That'll give the rest o' the shooters a chance." More guffaws. Luvella looked for Reeder and saw him, standing over to one side with Luke beside him. Her stomach lurched.

Mr. Johannson stood on the edge of the hotel's porch, so everyone could see him. "Ladies, Gentlemen, Young'uns, and you, too, Reeder!"

Luvella laughed with everyone, the visitors enjoying the camaraderie of the townspeople. *Mr. Johannson sure knows how to warm up a crowd.*

He continued, "You are about to witness our Annual Target Shoot, being held for the first time along with our first Annual Basket Bonanza."

Hoots and hollers and applause interrupted him.

"Here are the rules: There are six bottles up there for each contestant. Each contestant will use his own six-shooter and stand behind that line drawn in the dirt there." He pointed to just in front of where the line of contestants formed. "The one who shoots the most out of six bottles wins this Blue Ribbon here. Good luck to you all."

Everyone applauded. "Oh," Mr. Johannson added to the contestants, "don't shoot while Bill is putting up the bottles." Chuckles and comments rippled through the crowd. As the first contestant, Mr. Pearson, stood toe to the line, a quiet settled over everyone, and the mood turned serious, intense.

Mr. Pearson spread his legs in the dirt, shifting his weight from one to the other a few times, and then stood absolutely still, cocked his gun, aimed at the bottles, and shot. A bottle sprang into the air and sent tinkles of glass all around the fence. Everyone clapped their hands, and the men roared. Mr. Pearson smiled and waved to them. Then prepared for his second shot. In the end, he knocked three bottles down.

Mr. Melk was next: four bottles. Mr. Maartens: three bottles. Two visitors tried and each got two bottles. Soon it was Luvella's turn. She picked up the gun from the table, where Daddy had just put it for her, and was surprised again at how heavy it felt in her hands. She walked to the front, checked where the line was drawn in the dirt, placed her right toe near the line and her left foot, pointing sideways, behind her. Her balance felt steady.

She held the Colt, getting used to its heft, and cocked it. As she aimed, she was distracted for just a second by two things: Luke was watching her closely, and the bottles set up for her actually *were* smaller. She pulled her attention back to the gun's sights, aimed a tiny tad high, and squeezed the trigger. The sound of glass breaking was quick and small. Everyone inhaled, along with Luvella, as the first bottle, missing only the tip of its neck, teetered back and forth, back and forth, and finally fell to the ground. Everyone exhaled together and people shifted their feet.

*Not so high this time, Luvella,* she said to herself, cocked, aimed, and shot the gun. A splash of glass rewarded her. She cocked, aimed and shot four more times, each time bringing a spray of sparkles in the sunlight and the sound of tiny splintering chimes.

"And the winner of the Blue Ribbon award is…" Mr. Johannson boomed, "No surprise, folks, our very own Luvella Andersson!"

When she walked down the steps of the hotel porch, blue ribbon in hand, Luvella looked to where Reeder and Luke had been. They were wearing broad smiles. Luke whistled and Reeder waved both arms, then they clapped and clapped. Luvella waved back at them, and to many in the crowd, smiling. She gave the gun back to Daddy and returned to the caboose.

Bessie's face was the picture of pleasure as Luvella stepped into the store. "Luvella, I'm sure you've never had so much cash in this cash box before." She whispered as some women climbed the steps to the platform. "Everything tallies, and you have fifty-four dollars and thirty-two cents!" She squeezed Luvella's hands, pumping them up and down.

"Oh, my!" Luvella said. "Do I have anything left?" They laughed. "Bessie, go ahead back to Vanessa now. She'll be looking for her Mama. And thank you for helping me out today."

Everyone had agreed to close their businesses at four o'clock so the merchants could eat and enjoy the doings. Luvella had people in the caboose until about four-fifteen, but when she was ushering them out and putting the "Closed" sign in her front door, she heard a slight knock on her back door. She turned as the door opened. Luke stood there, looking taller and broader in the confines of the caboose, and even more handsome. He wore a white shirt, buttoned to the collar, a black tie, its short ends crossed at the top button of his shirt, and his black hair glistened, falling soft as corn silk around his ears.

"Luke!" She squealed and rushed to hug him just as she had Hannah. He hesitated for a moment. Then he wrapped his arms around her, lifting her off her feet. Luvella released his neck, starting to pull back to look at him, but he held her more tightly, bending his head. His head kept bending until his mouth found hers.

Luvella felt the fullness of his lips, as he softly brushed them against hers. Then she felt an urgency rush through his whole body. He pulled her against him and kissed her, hard. She let him kiss her, savored the sensation that shot down her and burrowed into her deepest parts. *What am I doing? This is not proper.*

She mustered every ounce of decorum she possibly

could and gently pushed herself away. Her face was on fire, she knew, and she still couldn't accept the feelings in the rest of her body.

When he set her down so her feet touched the floor, his eyes, dark and glittering, looked down at her. Then he grinned. She noticed how even his teeth were and that he had a cleft in his chin, like Uncle Isaac's.

"What's so funny?" she asked, pouting.

"You," he said, still standing close to her, his eyes searching her face. "You're glad to see me, huh?"

"Ohhhh!" she groaned. "There you go again. You just love to make me mad, don't you?" She turned around and stomped back to the desk.

He followed her. "No, I don't, Luvella. I like to tease you, yes. Just for fun. But I don't know why you get mad so easily."

Luvella closed and locked her cash box and put her ledger, pen, and ink bottle under the desk. "I don't know why, either," she said.

He leaned on the desk, bending near her. "Is this something you do to all the boys?" She snapped her eyes up at him, but he wasn't teasing. He was serious.

"There aren't boys. I'm too busy with my business." As soon as she said it, she wished she hadn't. "But when they did tease me—in school—I didn't bother to get mad. I just ignored them." She came out from behind the desk and walked around him toward the front.

"So I'm different?" he persisted.

Luvella stopped, stood still. She didn't hear a smirk in his voice, and she knew now that she should give him a good answer, that he was truly wondering about her. She turned to face him.

"Yes, Luke," she said softly. "You're different."

The expression that spilled across his face and turned his eyes into melted chocolate sent thunderbolts through her body, lodging in the pit of her stomach on top of what was already happening there. She wasn't sure what was going on, but a sense of propriety suddenly assaulted her, and she knew they should go out to the bonanza. Luke apparently was experiencing the same feeling. They left the caboose quietly, Luvella locking the doors behind them. As they crossed the road together to the hotel, she asked, "How did your"—she looked around them—"your…*trip* go?"

He quickly surveyed the people around, too. "I want to tell you about that, but not here."

Mr. Raven called Luke to help him with the wagon, and Luvella joined Anna and brought her over to meet Hannah. Anna gushed. "Oh, I was so afraid I'd never get to meet you, Hannah. You're just as pretty as Luvella said you were."

They talked about baby Matthew, giggled when Hannah said she wished Frank could take the baby's night feedings, and all took turns cuddling him. When Hannah went inside the hotel to feed Matthew, Anna took Luvella aside.

"Only one problem all day, Luvella," she said. "One girl—about fifteen, I'd say—said she wouldn't get on a hay wagon with an Indian driving." Anna started giggling. "And Reeder came over to the wagon, swept me up in his arms, and set me on the wagon, then he did the same to the girl. There were already several other people sitting around on the bales of hay. Reeder jumped up and sat next to that girl and told Mr. Raven to start up. Reeder was so handsome and grinned and winked at her that I think she completely forgot what she had said.

"And oh, Luvella! Reeder winked at me, too." She pretended she was going to faint. "I think I'm in love!"

"Ewwww! With Reeder? My brother?"

"Oh yes, Luvella. Look how handsome he is. And he's certainly a lot of fun. There's always laughing when Reeder's around." Her eyes sparkled.

"Yes, and there's usually trouble in the offing, too." Luvella laughed.

Mr. Melk began to pound heavy tongs against a large piece of metal. "Dinner! Dinner!" he shouted without a trace of his accent, then added, "Ven you hand in your tickets up on de porch, you vill get your plates."

Clusters of people sat on blankets to eat, on Mr. Smythe's porch, where he had set up several tables, and some people, mostly children, had even climbed back up on the wagons, using the hay for tables and some for chairs. Luvella peered from one group to another. Some were laughing, others talking seriously about some topic, but the general atmosphere was warm and friendly. *Good people together with good people,* she thought, smiling.

She searched for Luke, but didn't see him. She didn't see Reeder either and checked quickly the privy behind the depot. It was still intact.

The sales reports that the merchants passed from one to the other that afternoon showed that business was even better than they had expected. Some had sold out of their baskets, as well as some other items. She, herself, had only two baskets left at the caboose, and not one of the scented soaps was left. Her handmade sweaters were all gone, and her Penny Table was such a favorite that she decided to keep it as a regular offering.

Mama called her. "Help us redd the tables, Luvella? Time for dancing!"

Soon Mr. Johannson and Mr. Pearson were tapping their feet and fiddling away. The dance area on the road in front of the hotel was crowded. Luvella couldn't see Luke anywhere. *Where is he?* she wondered, feeling the anger rise.

"Luvella, may I have this dance?"

She turned around to see the Pearson boy smiling. She couldn't even remember his name! Oh, yes, it was Max. "All right, Max," she said. At least she'd get to dance.

He fumbled his very first step, but as Luvella guided him and smiled, he gradually moved with the music. Toward the end of the dance, as she twirled herself around, she saw Luke, leaning against the side of the hotel, watching her. She almost tripped.

Mr. Johannson announced a reel, and everyone lined up. Luke came over and with a hand at her back, steered her to the dance area, standing opposite her in line. She flashed a huge smile at him. She loved the reel, almost as much as she loved the waltz. The music started, and he reached for her hands and led her down the line. She remembered the similar dance they had done after Aunt Hilda's funeral. Luke had a strong sense of rhythm and moved easily to the music. Whenever they sashayed together between the two lines or met each other to dos-a-dos, their eyes met. Luvella wondered if her eyes matched the light in his when he looked at her. She felt as if they did.

All too soon, Mr. Johannson announced, "Last

dance, Folks. This one's a waltz."

Luke had wandered off again, and Luvella peered at the crowd. Hannah and Frank were dancing. Mrs. Raven was holding Matthew. She saw Reeder dancing with Anna and wondered what clues about them she had been missing of late.

An arm circled her back, a hand resting on her far shoulder, and Luke's resonant voice murmured in her ear. "Would you care to dance, miss?"

They swung into step immediately, swaying to the one-two-three rhythm together. He stepped to one side, back together, and spun her around, one-two-three.

"I had no idea you were such a good dancer, Luke. I would never have gotten mad at you if I'd known" She grinned up at him.

"I'm an Indian. I was born to it," he said, and twirled her around. They were next to Hannah and Frank.

Hannah said, "Oh Luke. You're doing everything I taught you. Good."

As Luke glowered playfully at Hannah, Luvella burst into laughter, missing a step. "Didn't you know, Hannah? He was born to it."

He finally chuckled. "So. You've found me out."

"Well, just that one little bit of you. I think there must be more, though."

They danced and smiled and poked fun at each other. As the final bars of the music played, Luke said, "After we get to your house, I'd like to walk with you for a little bit. Maybe to the creek behind your house?"

Luvella tried to act as if she did that every evening, but she knew her eyes gave her away. "I'll meet you on the porch. With both our mothers there, they probably won't need me to help with the leftovers."

As the crowd began separating into groups to go home, Mr. Johannson looked over to Luvella and asked discreetly, "You want me to tell them what we talked about?" After she nodded yes, he raised his fiddle and his voice to say, "Wait a minute, folks! We've been hearing that lots of you would like to visit us this winter. We could have a winter festival—with sleigh rides, ice skating, snowman contests, plus pretty much what we had today. Except we'd have to eat inside the hotel." Everyone laughed. "Who would like a winter festival?" Whistles and hoorays and applause filled the air.

"That's good, folks. Watch your newspapers and *Harper's Magazine* for information. I think maybe sometime in January would be a good time.

"And now it's good night. Thank you all for coming and celebrating our Basket Bonanza with us. Have a safe trip home, and we hope to see you this winter."

Wagons were loaded with their passengers. Reeder asked if he could stay behind and help Mr. Smythe with some clean-up work, which didn't fool anybody. They'd all seen him dancing with Anna. He said, "I'll ride Daisy home. She'd just be tagging along behind the wagon anyway."

Luvella thought she saw Daddy wink at Reeder, but she wasn't sure.

Suddenly, Luke said, a note of alarm raising his voice, "Reeder. Wait up!" He was pointing across the road, toward Luvella's store.

## Chapter Twenty-Five

"Smoke! Over behind the caboose," Luke shouted as he ran across the road.

"No!" Luvella screamed, running after Luke. "Daisy's there!"

As if in response, a terrified whinny came from the back of the caboose. Luke and Reeder were already ahead of Luvella, their long legs devouring the road.

Somebody yelled, "Get your buckets!"

"Daisy! Here, Girl!" Luvella called. She ran around the caboose where Reeder was leading a wild-eyed Daisy to safety. Luvella tugged Daisy's lead back to the hotel and gave the horse to Anna to tether.

Returning to the caboose, Luvella's heart stopped. A long lick of flame spiked toward the sky from behind her store. She zig-zagged among the men, each carrying buckets of water, to the back platform. Hisses and steam filled the air as each pail of water doused the flames and drowned the smoking embers.

Reeder grabbed Luke's arm. "I just saw someone in the woods. Luke, run to the mountain road, at the end of these woods, and wait for him in case I don't catch him. Lars, can you get Dushore's sheriff before he leaves here?"

Both Luke and Reeder disappeared, leaving air and space where they had just been beating out the fire.

Half an hour later, Daddy declared the fire out and

the caboose safe. “It looks like we got to it fast enough to keep the damage low, Luvella.” He had his arm around her shoulders, hugging her to him. “Thanks to Luke’s keen smeller.”

She knew he was trying to lighten her mood. He continued, “With all the iron there, looks like we’ll only have to rebuild the platform and refinish that door.”

Shouting from the road grabbed their attention. Reeder and Luke were handing over Mr. Bocke to Dushore’s sheriff. Mr. Bocke, face smudged and the crown of his derby charred, begged the sheriff to take him away, to protect him from “these ruffians.”

The sheriff retorted, “Oh, don’t worry, sir. I’ll keep you away from them—and a good many other people.”

Mr. Harley, still holding a pail, said, “Thanks, Sheriff, for letting me know about Mr. Bocke’s forged warehouse receipts. I knew I shouldn’t have given him the cash. At least I didn’t give him the whole five hundred dollars.”

He turned to Luvella and Mr. Johannson as he joined them. “I didn’t have time to tell you today, Lars. The sheriff checked on that carload of cotton and told me that our Mr. Bocke must have forged those receipts he gave me. He doesn’t own any bales of cotton, let alone a carload.”

Mr. Johannson grinned down at Luvella. “Looks like it’s just you and the railroad, Luvella.”

****

Everyone was subdued on the ride home. Hannah and Frank and little Matthew rode in Mr. and Mrs. Raven’s wagon. Luke jumped in next to Luvella and rode in the back of her wagon with Mama. Daddy and Bill rode on the driver’s bench.

Mr. Raven, driving right behind the Andersson wagon, said, “Luvella, everyone tells me that you’re the person behind this whole Basket Bonanza. You are quite a remarkable young lady.” He glanced at Luke, then continued. “I managed to squeeze through the people there in your caboose to see your store, and you sure have a nice collection of things to sell. No wonder you were so popular today.”

Luke leaned toward Luvella, his arm touching her shoulder, sending shivers through her, and said, loud enough for everyone to hear, “I told him to say nice things to you.”

They all chuckled, settling into a mellow mood. Matthew had fallen asleep with the rocking of the wagon and at the laughter, Luvella saw him wriggle in Hannah’s arms, then snuggle down again.

“Really, Uncle Isaac came up with the baskets idea,” Luvella said, still talking to the Ravens, who were close behind them. “I was trying to think of some theme for a festival, and he said he could get lots of baskets for us to sell. That’s just the idea I needed.”

Bill said from the front of thc wagon. “Luvella, you must have really cleaned up today. I swear I saw more people going and coming at the caboose than anywhere else.” All the others nodded.

“I did sell almost everything,” Luvella answered. “Now I have to beg people to bring me some more replacements.”

Mrs. Raven leaned forward from her bench seat. “Well, I crochet pretty well, Luvella, and I noticed the people from out of town loved the Muncee things.”

Luvella shook her head yes in quick nods and laughed. “Yes! I think they thought they were getting something from the wild, wild west."

After more chuckles, Mrs. Raven said, "Well, I could make some prettier Indian dolls, too, dolls that you could charge more than two cents for."

"Mrs. Raven, any time you have some things made, whether it's sweaters, doilies, baskets, dolls, or anything else, just have someone bring them to me. Give me an idea of how much you want me to pay you, and when they're sold, I'll get the money back to you." Luvella was grateful for the business talk. It helped to calm her down from the fire and thinking about the walk she was going to have with Luke.

"Maybe Uncle Isaac would like to come visit us again. He wouldn't be breaking his mourning period if he were delivering things, would he?"

"Yes, how is Uncle Isaac managing?" Mama asked, leaning forward from her hay seat. "I was hoping he would be here for the bonanza."

"He misses Aunt Hilda, but he keeps busy and then spends a lot of time in the woods, I think probably praying." Mrs. Raven leaned forward again. "He talks about you a lot, Luvella. Says you remind him of his Hilda, that you look like her across the eyes, and you have her spunk."

"Ha!" Luke roared, as Matthew stirred again. "Spunk and then some!" He grinned down at Luvella and she giggled in spite of herself.

The conversation, warm, comfortable, faded as they climbed the mountain. The sun's low rays beamed out across the road like stripes from between the trees. At home, everyone took a job and the horses, wagons, and leftovers were taken care of in minutes.

Mrs. Raven told Luvella to "go along," that she and

Mama could finish cleaning up from the picnic. So Luvella went out to the porch where Luke was leaning against the railing, waiting for her. He smiled as she came out, scanning the group of men there before she saw him.

They fell into step, walking past the back of the house on a path that led to the creek. Their hands touched often as they swung their arms, each touch sending tiny chills through Luvella. They crossed the footbridge, Luvella clinging tightly to Luke's arm with one hand and the rope railing with the other as she went. She never forgot the time she had fallen into the creek that spring, years ago, and nearly drowned.

On the other side of the creek, Luke motioned to a boulder on which he had folded a saddle blanket earlier, making a comfortable seat for the two of them. Luvella sat obediently, her heart making loud thumps that she was afraid he could surely hear.

An orange-red beam from the sun danced on the rippled surface of the creek. Luvella glanced up to the sky and saw a few crimson clouds floating sleepily by, but one small cloud, over to the west, caught her interest. She pointed to it. "I think that's holding my nephew, Junior," she said softly to Luke, feeling confident that he wouldn't ridicule her for believing that. "He died from the typhoid. I thought poor Bessie would never get over losing him.

"But there are some days, I just know he's up there, watching us and laughing. Today was one of those days."

"Sometimes you sound like a Muncee, Luvella." He was smiling at her.

"Sometimes now I feel like a Muncee." She

laughed.

He shifted on the blanket to face her and took one of her hands. Her heart exploded. "You asked how my vision quest was." He looked down at her hand, held it up against his and smiled. Her fingertips came to just the first knuckle of his fingers. "As I had feared, it took me a while to concentrate, to forget you." He rested his elbows on his knees, holding her hand in both of his now.

"But I finally was able to make two decisions before I went home from my quest." He stood and paced in front of Luvella. "When I found you in the woods, so sick, so hurt, I wanted to make you better. I wanted to heal you. When you actually *did* feel better after I took care of you, I felt…I just felt like I wanted to do it again, to make someone who's been sick well. This was different from when I helped the doctor at Carlisle. This was just me making the decisions. I knew I wanted to be a doctor."

He looked at her, as if for approval. Luvella thought a moment. "Luke, I remember how careful, how gentle you were with me. You were, really, just like a doctor, now that I think about it. In fact, you know we never did call a doctor for my ankle. You were my doctor. But how are you going to be one?"

He appeared pleased at her question. He moved closer to her on the blanket. "There's this doctor in Hughsville…" he began.

"Dr. Jordan!" Luvella interrupted. "He came from Hughsville every week to take care of Daddy and Reeder and Bill when they had typhoid fever. And Mama. Daddy just talked to him on Mr. Pearson's store telephone a few weeks ago. Mama had pneumonia, remember?"

"Yes, his name is Dr. Jordan. So you know him?" His eyes lit up with another connection established between them. "Well, he has agreed to have me work with him. His training will be very valuable. As I work with him, he'll go through the text books with me so I can take the exams at the school. I already have the recommendation from Carlisle's doctor, from when I worked in Carlisle's clinic helping him. Of course, I'll have to attend some classes at Albany, too, to get a degree." Luke leaned his elbows on his knees again.

"Dr. Jordan knows I'm a Muncee, but he says he needs help, nobody else wants to be available for doctoring twenty-four hours a day, and he's willing to train me and teach me if I'm willing to follow him around at all hours."

"Oh my goodness!" Luvella said. "You are really very fortunate, Luke, and I know first-hand that you'll make a really good doctor. But Hughsville is so far away—even farther away than Forksville." She looked up at him, wanted to say *Will I ever see you again?* but thought that would be far too forward of her.

"Yes, it is. And I may not be able to get back home, or to Muncy Valley"—he watched her—"for maybe two years, at least. Dr. Jordan just might let me come home for a spell when things are quiet in Hughsville, but I can't plan on that. And then I'll be away for at least another year at medical school."

Luvella was too busy thinking to say anything. Finally she remembered his vision quest. "You said you had made two decisions," she said. "What was the other one?"

He peered at her, intently, his eyes like melted

chocolate again. "The other one is about you," he said, a sudden huskiness in his voice. "I've made a decision, but it depends on your answer to my question."

Luvella almost wished she hadn't asked. She felt so nervous, and she could feel his…fear? He reached for her hand again, covered it with both his, and kept squeezing it and patting it. *He's nervous, too.*

"Look, Luvella, I know I'm a lot older than you are…"

"You are not a lot older than I am," she interrupted heatedly. "You're only eighteen, two years older."

"All right, just two years older in years. But I wasn't brought up in a home, with parents who really cared about what happened to me. I was practically imprisoned in a government school by people who only wanted to scratch out any Indian"—he accented the word—"traits or traditions I might have. When they were through with me, they would have opened the gates and let me out to find my own way back home, miles away." He let go of her hands and crossed one leg over his other knee.

"As it turned out, their Infirmary needed someone to help the doctor there—which is where I learned a lot about medicine already—and Pop Warner wanted to build a winning football team. I'd been on the team two years, so I agreed to stay on for another couple years." He sat up straight again and turned toward her.

"That's what I mean by older, Luvella. I've been out in a rough world. The only good thing about that boarding school was that I did get a good education, even beyond high school, and a lot of medical training."

"I'm sorry, Luke. That must have been awful. I can't imagine growing up without Mama and Daddy and my brothers, even though Reeder is a terror sometimes."

Luke chuckled. "Ayup. But I really like him." He knit his fingers through Luvella's. "The other decision I made was about you, as I said. I know what I want to do for my life's work—doctoring—and I know I'd like to have you with me." He held their clasped hands up and examined them, then put them down again. "For the rest of my life." He whispered it.

"But like I just said…" He cleared his throat. "It may be three or four years before I can start working as a doctor on my own." He let go of her hand and folded his together. "I'd like to hear about how you are, Luvella, how your life is, and I'd like to tell you about mine. If I wrote you letters regularly, would you write me back? Would you…spend your free time with me, at least by mail? And then, think about the rest of your life?"

He had said what had been on his mind and he sighed now, obviously relieved. Luvella sighed, too, searching for the words to answer him.

"I haven't written very many letters in my life, but I think writing you would be easy. I'd kind of like to tell you about how my store is coming along, and about my trip to Pittsburgh for the Chamber convention, and you're the only person I really feel easy talking to about my mountain." She hunched her shoulders up to her ears, smiled at him, and let her shoulders down. "Yes, I'll write you back."

"*Faithfully*?" he asked. "I mean, would you forget that Pearson fella and…wait for me?"

Luvella looked at him, waiting for his grin, but he was inspecting her face. And his was very serious, emphasizing what he said.

"Yes, Luke, I will write you. You know"—she looked down at her hands and raised her eyes back up to meet his—"I have no interest in Max Pearson or any other boy. And yes, I'll wait for you." She knew, at his look of relief, that she had said what he wanted to hear and what he had had a difficult time asking her.

A light splash from down creek brought their attention to that direction. "Hmmm, guess it's time for the animals to come for their evening drink. I'd better get you back to the house. But first…"

He cupped his hands on either side of her face and gently lifted it as he bent his head. His lips caressed hers. He pulled her close to him and wrapped his arms around her. His mouth seized hers, pressing, demanding. His hands crushed her against him as a small groan escaped him. Luvella responded, with all the naturalness inherent in a woman.

He released her, while she was still trying to breathe, to stop the pounding in her heart. Then he stood and pulled her to her feet, keeping a tight hold of her hand.

"I want you to be mine, Luvella, forever." He held her shoulders and bent to give her another kiss, light and quick. He led her back to the house.

Just as they walked from the bridge, Reeder rode up on Daisy. He was whistling and spread a grin clear across his face when he saw them. "Ah, 'tis a lovely night, 'tisn't it?" He sighed.

Luvella put her hands on her hips. "Reeder, don't you go breaking Anna's heart or I'll…I'll…"

Reeder had jumped off Daisy, slapping her rump so she'd walk into the barn, and ambled over to Luke and

Luvella. "Sis," he said softly, pointing his finger at her, "you girls can break the boys' hearts too, you know."

Luvella was speechless, for once. She had just seen a rare, emotional side of Reeder. She couldn't wait to talk to Anna tomorrow. Reeder tipped his hat back on his head and walked to the barn to bed down Daisy. Luke and Luvella continued to the porch.

"I'll see you tomorrow morning before we leave," he said. "Good night, Luvella."

"Good night, Luke." She walked into the kitchen somehow. She couldn't feel the floor under feet. Mama, Daddy, and the Ravens were all looking at her, but she couldn't talk to them. How could she? She was in Heaven, or in some special place where nobody talked; they just smiled.

"Luvella." Mama's voice brought her back and she looked at them all around the table. Matthew was sleeping in his basket on the floor, next to where Hannah and Frank were sitting. "Come sit with us."

"Oh! Yes, Mama," she said, and Hannah giggled at her.

Luke and Reeder came in together, Luke's eyes finding Luvella's immediately. Hannah caught the look and leaned over to squeeze Luvella's hand under the table. They smiled at each other.

Daddy said, "Ayup. We'll be going to Forksville in two weeks." Mr. and Mrs. Raven nodded, with big smiles. Daddy continued," Want to come with us? We'll leave late on Saturday and come back Sunday, when our businesses will be closed."

"Oh, that's wonderful, Daddy!" Luvella squealed. "We can see Uncle Isaac again. And can we teach Mama and Daddy how to dance Muncee-style?" She looked at Hannah and Mrs. Raven. Everyone laughed. The Ravens said, “We’ll see.”

Luke spoke up, looking at his parents. “I won’t be there,” he said, “two weeks from now.”

Mama and Daddy stared at him while Mr. and Mrs. Raven beamed. Luke explained how he was going to study to be a doctor, that Dr. Jordan had wanted him to be there last Monday, but gave Luke permission to help his parents with the bonanza first. Luke would be leaving for Hughsville Monday morning.

Luke finished by saying, “I think maybe I’ve always wanted to be a doctor, but helping to heal Luvella’s wounds, that time in the woods, really made me think I should be a doctor.”

Hannah interjected, “He was probably born to it, like he was to dancing.”

Luvella and Hannah and Frank all burst into laughter as Luke bent his head, grinning and shaking it back and forth. He looked at his and Luvella’s parents. “I got caught in a fib to Luvella.”

The conversation and smiles and laughter went on until late evening, when Mama said that no one would wake up in the morning if they didn’t get to sleep soon. Luvella curled up on the davenport after everyone else had gone upstairs, and the boys out to the barn. Once, during the night, she heard Matthew cry for a few minutes. Then Hannah’s bare feet padded on the floor and Matthew was quiet. Luvella knew Hannah was feeding him.

In the morning, Luvella got up as soon as she heard people stir upstairs. She washed up at the kitchen sink and quickly dressed into the blue calico dress she had laid out on the chair next to the davenport. She was making the coffee when Mama came down the stairs.

She helped Mama prepare breakfast until Mrs. Raven came down, then Luvella was relegated to setting the table. Bacon was sizzling, coffee perking, potatoes and eggs frying and crackling in the hot bacon grease. Luvella could smell Mama's bread from yesterday as she warmed it on the stovetop. Daddy and Mr. Raven came down the stairs and headed out toward the privy.

All of a sudden, Luvella heard hoots and hollers and the thumping of heavy footsteps running out in back. She went to the door, but Daddy, grinning from ear to ear, said, "No, you stay inside. Luke is in the altogether chasing Reeder. I guess Reeder took Luke's clothes from beside the creek."

Frank said, "I've got to see this!" and ran outside.

Daddy added, "I suspect Reeder will be in the creek in a few minutes. He's finally met his match." He and Mr. Raven guffawed as Reeder yelped, and the sound of loud splashes came from the creek. Luvella thought she heard Mr. Raven say to Daddy, "Young bucks in love."

Soon, Bill came in to get a dry outfit for Reeder. And later still, all the men came in for breakfast. Luke's and Reeder's heads were dripping water, leaving their shirts wet across their shoulders.

"Next time, I'll hide my clothes really good, like in a bear's den." Luke grinned at Reeder.

"And I'll find 'em and get away, so you'll never get me in the creek again," Reeder poked Luke's arm.

Mr. Raven said, "At the government school, Luke found out from the Apaches there that they bathe daily in their rivers and streams, even in the winter. He likes the idea, I guess, 'cuz he does it all the time."

Luvella smiled, thinking, *Well, now I know it* is *an Indian tradition, not necessarily a Muncee tradition.*

After breakfast, Mama wouldn't let Mrs. Raven or Hannah help clean up. "Luvella and I will do it in no time after you leave," she said, putting her arm around Luvella's shoulders. The men had harnessed the horses to the wagon and loaded the satchels of clothing and the lunches Mama had fixed for them into it.

Finally, it was time to say goodbye. As Mama and Mrs. Raven were hugging, Luke walked next to Luvella and said quietly, "Goodbye, Luvella. Don't forget…me."

"I won't, Luke," she answered. "I promise." Then he went to the wagon and climbed on the driver's bench next to his father. Luvella and Hannah embraced while everyone said "goodbye, we'll see you soon now," "thank you for coming," or "thank you for your hospitality…" Mr. Raven slapped the reins lightly on the horses' rumps and the wagon lurched forward.

As they pulled out of the Anderssons' drive and went down the mountain road, Luke's eyes constantly smiled at Luvella. She stood there, even after the wagon was out of sight, feeling Luke's warmth. Going back into the house, she stopped to look at the mountain around her, inhaling its peace. From the adjoining woods, the sun glinted low, winking through the trees the promise of another beautiful day.

*The Power of the East, rising to greet Father Sky,* Luvella thought. She studied the sky above, still gossamery in anticipation.

*Thank you for our perfect bonanza.* She contemplated the pines, with their branches stretched in their upturned arcs and their abundance coursing to the top of the mountain. *Even my caboose was spared serious damage.*

As if in sympathy, a gray cloud floated over the mountain crest. Luvella twisted her mouth to one side. *All these good things happening...Luke. Ahhh, Luke... And I have lots and lots of work and planning ahead of me now, for the Chamber of Commerce trip to Pittsburgh and for my business.* A shiver of joy ran through her and she rubbed each arm with the other hand vigorously.

*But first, I think I'll write a letter.* She smiled and went into the house.

## A word about the author…

Joan Foley Baier is the author of *Luvella's Promise*, a children's novel, *Roar of Revenge*, an adult e-book novella, and many published short stories and essays for both children and adults. She lives quietly in Rochester, New York, with family, friends, and books close by.

You can visit her website at www.joanbaier.com.

Thank you for purchasing
this publication of The Wild Rose Press, Inc.

If you enjoyed the story, we would appreciate your
letting others know by leaving a review.

For other wonderful stories,
please visit our on-line bookstore at
www.thewildrosepress.com.

For questions or more information
contact us at
info@thewildrosepress.com.

The Wild Rose Press, Inc.
www.thewildrosepress.com

Stay current with The Wild Rose Press, Inc.

Like us on Facebook

https://www.facebook.com/TheWildRosePress

And Follow us on Twitter
https://twitter.com/WildRosePress